Second C SEALs Next Door

Forbidden Reverse Harems of Harmony Valley: Book One

An Age Gap Military Reverse Harem Romance

Summer Haze

© Copyright 2024 by Summer Haze – All rights reserved.
1. Edition

Title: Second Chance SEALs Next Door
ISBN: 9798323691586
Author: Summer Haze
Publisher: Pure Passion Reads GmbH, Uferstr. 3a, 39307 Roßdorf

In no way is it legal to reproduce, duplicate, or transmit any part of this document in either electronic means or in printed format. Recording of this publication is strictly prohibited and any storage of this document is not allowed unless with written permission from the publisher. All rights reserved.

Respective publisher owns all copyrights not held by the author.

CONTENTS

Chapter 1	8
Chapter 2	13
Chapter 3	18
Chapter 4	24
Chapter 5	29
Chapter 6	34
Chapter 7	41
Chapter 8	46
Chapter 9	51
Chapter 10	56
Chapter 11	61
Chapter 12	69
Chapter 13	74
Chapter 14	81
Chapter 15	87
Chapter 16	93
Chapter 17	98
Chapter 18	104

Chapter 19	109
Chapter 20	114
Chapter 21	120
Chapter 22	127
Chapter 23	134
Chapter 24	140
Chapter 25	145
Chapter 26	150
Chapter 27	155
Chapter 28	163
Chapter 29	168
Chapter 30	173
Chapter 31	178
Chapter 32	183
Chapter 33	188
Chapter 34	193
Chapter 35	198
Chapter 36	203
Chapter 37	207
Chapter 38	212

Chapter 39	216
Chapter 40	223
Chapter 41	228
Chapter 42	233
Chapter 43	238
Chapter 44	244
Chapter 45	249
Epilogue	256
Thank You	261
About the Author	262

CHAPTER 1
Violet

If the men in town knew that *Good, Clean Fun* was a front for a much rowdier business, they didn't show it. On the rare occasion one of them did wander into the store, they never would've ventured past the closed door at the back. The soap and candle store in the front was cute and the products were great, but it was the secrets behind that door in the back which brought in women from all over Harmony Valley. *Doll's*, as it'd been named along the way, was a store and meeting place just for the women around town. Margaret James had started it when women were outnumbered by men six to one in the valley and she'd grown sick of hearing men talk all day long. Doll's was a well-kept secret which acted as one-part social club and one part sex-positive experience.

Was it strange that a seventy-year-old woman ran a secret speakeasy which had walls lined with more sex toys than most people would ever see in their lives? Maybe. Was Margaret's age a hindrance when it came time for local women to take care of themselves by buying a few top-of-the-line toys and rant about their male counterparts over a cup of espresso? Not even a little bit. *Doll's* was pink, frilly, and lush, a place no one ever would've imagined existing in the valley between the Harmony and Stairway Mountains. It was a little slice of heaven amidst the most beautiful nature scenery that could be found anywhere in the country.

I hadn't moved to Lilyfield explicitly for *Good, Clean Fun*, or its sexy backend, *Doll's*. It'd been a little of everything that drew me in. Margaret was a big part, the views another. Then, there was the close community of women, close enough to hold a secret like *Doll's* tight to their chests. There was also my personal history with Harmony Valley. I'd only ever spent two nights in the valley six years earlier, but those two nights were all it took to hook me. Almost every day I'd spent living with my parents back home in Kansas, had been filled with thoughts of the valley and its inhabitants.

I was now officially one of its residents and my heart already felt lighter. I'd been welcomed to town right as the leaves were starting to change color and the days were becoming cooler. Seeing the valley in the beginning of fall was unlike anything I'd ever experienced, and I was already madly in love.

Lily Elementary had been decorated with large leaves all along the interior walls with each child's name printed on them as I'd lead my son down the hallway to meet his teacher. He was starting a month late, but he was smart and made friends easily, so I knew he'd be fine. Forrest, named after the very trees surrounding Lilyfield, had greeted his teacher like he was twenty-six instead of six.

Ms. Jenny had been smitten right away. Forrest was like that, always instantly winning people over. He had three new best friends before we left the building that day.

When Margaret called me a month ago, I'd been bogged down with fatigue, the same fatigue I'd felt for over six years. When I'd found out I was pregnant with Forrest, I'd lived with my parents and listened to their ideas of what was best for me. I'd left college with only one semester outstanding before I graduated and I went straight to work at my parents' insurance company. It was fine. Everything was fine. Except, it wasn't. So, when Margaret called and told me she had a home and a job for me, I'd jumped at the chance to leave Kansas.

I'd met Margaret just after I found out I was pregnant and she had put me up in her own living room for the night and held me while I cried. I'd been looking for the father, without any real knowledge of where he was, but I'd come up empty-handed. Margaret had taken me into *Doll's*, given me a sex toy she said would help me relax, and fed me until I felt like I'd burst. She'd saved me then and she'd saved me again with that phone call a month earlier.

I would work at the only restaurant in Harmony Valley, a diner aptly named, *The One and Only*. I'd live in an apartment over a garage, for free, as long as I walked the owner's dogs twice a day. Margaret had made those promises and she'd kept them. I'd been in Lilyfield for two weeks and I'd already settled into my job at *The One and Only,* and in the apartment over the garage. Forrest loved his school. I'd already hung out with Margaret and several other women in town at *Doll's*. I was settling in. Things were already so much better than they'd been in Kansas.

I just hadn't met the owners of the house, yet. Or the

dogs. The owners were out of town and they'd boarded the dogs since they hadn't known when I'd arrive. No one appeared to know when they'd be back and Margaret seemed especially coy about the whole thing. I was halfway convinced I was crashing at someone's house without them knowing, but Joanie Cartwright, the owner of the diner, promised me it was all above board.

Everything seemed too good to be true. Between the free apartment and the amazing support group I'd instantly found, I couldn't help wondering when the other shoe would drop. I wasn't typically so pessimistic, but something about the last six years of my life had left me doubting good things. Although, after six years, maybe I *was* just a pessimist.

I didn't want anything about Harmony Valley to be off. I wanted a picture-perfect town with good friends and a good school for Forrest. I wanted us to be happy. Lilyfield had always somehow felt like home and once I'd changed the mailing address on my one credit card to Lilyfield, I was committed. Nothing could ruin it for me. Nothing.

That's what I told myself as I stared at the empty house day after day. It was a large house. It looked like the house from that old Steve Martin movie, *Father of the Bride*. A large white house with shutters and a manicured lawn, and flower boxes on the windows. The apartment over the garage was nicer than my parents' house back in Kansas.

What kind of people lived in such a beautiful home and just left it for weeks at a time? I couldn't imagine. *Where were they*, I wondered? I tried to imagine the fantastic vacation they were on, but I'd barely ever been anywhere, so I couldn't picture it. I could only picture the pretty house with the flower boxes. Forrest deserved a home like that. I promised myself I'd give him something similar one day. I didn't think I'd get it while waitressing at *The One and Only*, but I was doing okay for us, and without my parents' help, something they hadn't believed I could do.

It was my curiosity about the house which kept me watching it nightly. I felt like I was waiting, holding my breath, for the owners to show up. I didn't know why I felt so on edge about them, but I tried to chalk it up to nerves about meeting new bosses. Technically, that's what they'd be. They had to be nice people, surely; they had dogs. Dog people were great.

Night after night, I looked out at the house and wondered how long it would be until I spotted them. I hoped they liked me. I hoped they really were nice. I hoped, more than anything, that everything didn't prove to be too good to be true.

I did a lot of hoping and watching and that was why, when I heard something crash behind the house right before Forrest's bedtime, I was ready. I'd been waiting for something to happen for nearly two weeks and it seemed like the time for things to happen, had come.

CHAPTER 2
Violet

The crashing sound startled me enough that I jumped up from my window seat in the living room and swung a wide-eyed glance at Forrest. He had his head buried in a book and didn't even look up. I looked back down at the house and swallowed. The lights in the house were all still off. If it was the owners making sounds, surely they'd turn lights on. I debated what to do for a few seconds before I grabbed the closest thing I had to a weapon, Forrest's wiffle ball bat, and inched towards the door. If someone was breaking in, I had to do something. My free stay would surely be over if I didn't try to stop a break-in.

"I'm going to run downstairs and check on something, Forrest. Stay here." I gripped the doorknob and made sure he looked up at me. "I mean it. Stay up here. Okay?"

He frowned. "Why do you have my bat?"

I heard another sound and gripped the bat tighter. "Just stay up here. If you come down, you'll be grounded until you're fifty."

Without waiting for a response, I slipped out of the door and down the stairs. The stairs were on the far side of the garage, which gave the apartment an even greater sense of privacy, but as I crept down, I couldn't help wishing the stairs were inside the garage so I could have a few more minutes of feeling sheltered. I made sure to step over the last stair because it squeaked every time it was stepped on.

Feeling like an absolute knob, I tip-toed my way around the garage and let myself into the fenced-in front yard through the gate. I hadn't been inside the yard and I was momentarily distracted by how plush the grass felt under my bare feet. What the hell kind of grass were they growing that felt like pillows? I took another few steps and then yelped when a shrill cry rang through the night. I'd stepped on a squeaky toy.

Frozen in place, I glared down at the rubber chicken and prayed no one heard it. My prayers fell on deaf ears, though, because just as I was trying to lift my foot, I heard what sounded like a stampede coming at me. I looked up in horror and waited for my sudden death. It sounded like a group of men were running my way, so I squeezed my eyes shut and waited for the moment they spotted me, but instead, I just felt warm air on my chest. I opened my eyes in panic, thinking some creepy man was breathing on my chest, but what I saw was much better.

A giant dog was standing in front of me, looking up at me with the silliest expression on his face. I assumed he was a male dog because of the boob fascination, but I was just guessing at that point. The dog was the size of a horse and he looked identical to *Scooby Doo*. I tilted my head to look at him and he tilted his in the other direction to look back at me. Then he leaned forward and ran his giant tongue over my chest and neck, leaving behind a trail of drool.

"Oh, man! Buddy, that's a lot of drool. As much as I appreciate a good kiss, I'm not into the wet ones." I let him sniff my hand, got a few more wet kisses, and then gently petted him. "You're soft. Someone takes good care of you, don't they? Did you break in? Huh? Are you the one who broke in? Yeah?"

I'd quickly defaulted into high-pitched happy dog talk. I couldn't help myself. I loved animals and the dog in front of me seemed especially lovable. I'd forgotten all about the idea of someone breaking in for real. I scratched the dog behind the ears, happy the giant was such a good boy.

A high-pitched barking filled the air and then there was a small dog at my feet, jumping up on my knees. He, again I was really making some assumptions about their genders, was as small as the other one was large. Without thinking, I bent down and scooped the little guy into my arms. He stuck his tongue into my ear and then yipped practically against my eardrum.

"Ouch, puppers! I need the use of that ear. Mind not screaming directly into it?"

I'd dropped the bat at some point and my guard was fully down, so when a deep male voice spoke from the shadows next to the fence, I used the only defense I had. I screamed at the top of my lungs. The dogs joined me and the three of us created quite the ruckus together.

"General. Captain. Quiet!" A different masculine voice called out abruptly, and then it was just me screaming. "You, too, woman. Quiet."

I snapped my lips closed and clutched the small dog to

my chest. "Who are you and why are you here? These are attack dogs. Come any closer and they'll eat your face off. Ever seen a man without a face? One wrong move and that's your life, pal."

"You just heard me give those dogs commands. You really think you can threaten me with them?" The second voice spoke again, sounding amused rather than murderous. "To answer your first question, we own this house. That's who we are *and* why we're here. Who are *you* and why are *you* here?"

Feeling foolish and wishing I'd kept my nosy self upstairs in my apartment, I cleared my throat and put the small dog down. I grabbed the bat while I was bent over and clutched it to my side while backing away. "I'm the new tenant over the garage. I'm really sorry. I heard something and assumed someone was breaking in. Obviously, that's not the case, so I'll just be on my way."

A third voice spoke from not too far away. "You thought you heard someone breaking in so you grabbed a plastic bat and ran down to take care of it?"

I frowned. "Yes. I don't exactly keep other weapons on hand."

"*Other* weapons would imply the bat you're holding is a weapon." The first voice sounded like laughter was imminent. "Turn the floodlights on, Ben."

I wasn't a fan of being laughed at and I'd just remembered I was wearing my pajamas and a face mask, so I had no desire to hang around. "Well, I should get back to the apartment. Maybe we can meet under—"

The lights flashed on and after a second of being blinded by the brightness, I felt like I'd been kicked in the stomach. All the breath left me and I stumbled back a few steps, setting off that damn squeaky chicken again. My heart hammered painfully in my chest as I saw the owners of the house for the first time. Only it wasn't the first time I'd ever seen them.

They were three very familiar faces from six years earlier. I'd searched for them then, but I'd given up hope of ever finding them. As I stood there, staring, I knew too much time and life had passed for finally finding them to be a good thing.

So, I did the only thing I could think of. I hoped they didn't recognize me under the mask, if they even remembered me, and I started backing away faster. Escape was now my goal.

CHAPTER 3
Violet

"*Stop*." Benjamin, seemingly still the stoic one, stared across the fence at me with a fierce gaze.

I let out an awkward laugh and tugged at my pajama top. "You know what they say. Early to bed, early to rise… Early bird gets the worm. I'll just be on my way."

"Violet." Mason, who stood closest to me, swept his gaze over my figure in its entirety.

I cleared my throat and considered lying. I was panicking and I didn't do well while panicking. I couldn't think straight. Even if I believed lying would help me, I couldn't think of a lie to save my life. "Um. Yes?"

Justin had been the most forward all those years ago and nothing had changed. He easily hopped the fence and walked right up to me. Standing so close, I could see the gold inside his hazel eyes. "What the hell are you doing here? How are you here?"

I blinked up at him, momentarily taken aback by how

handsome he still was. That was why I sounded like an idiot when I answered. "I live here now. I walk the dogs."

Benjamin moved closer. "What are you doing in Lilyfield?"

It was the sound of small feet shuffling across pavement that broke my stupor. I couldn't let them see Forrest. Not yet, at least. I needed a plan. I needed a moment to think. I spun around and rushed towards the gate, but Benjamin caught my arm.

"The least you could do is give us an explanation, Violet." He didn't understand I was barely able to form two thoughts, much less words. He was asking for too much.

I tried to tug myself free but it was too late. The sound of the gate opening behind me snapped my focus to one singular point: Forrest. "Go back upstairs, Forrest. Now."

"Whoa! Is that a dog or a horse? Wow!" Ignoring me completely, Forrest hurried over to where the dogs were sitting and watching the back and forth between the humans. "Can I pet your dogs? Mommy told me to always ask first. I asked, so, can I pet them?"

Benjamin's grip on my arm tightened, not enough to hurt, but enough to let me know he wasn't blind to what was unfolding before him. I heard his breathing change, becoming ragged, and when I dared a glance up at him, his eyes were drinking Forrest in.

I cleared my throat. "Good job asking, buddy, but you heard what I said. Go back upstairs and wait for me. You weren't supposed to come down to begin with, were you?"

With his hand out, waiting to pet the larger dog, he looked back at me. "You screamed! Grandpa said I'm the man of the house now. That means I have to take care of you when you scream. Grandpa said so."

I pried Ben's fingers from my arm and hurried over to kneel in front of Forrest. I just needed him to go back upstairs. Some idiotic part of my brain was convinced that if I put him away fast enough, it would be like the guys never saw him. "You're six, baby. You've got a little while before you have to worry about protecting me. How about you go back upstairs and you can meet the puppies tomorrow? I'll read you *Harry Potter* again if you're in bed and tucked in when I get up there."

"But, Mom!" He giggled as the big dog licked his hand. "Please, let me play with them!"

I swallowed down as much panic as I could and tried to speak to him as calmly as possible. "Forrest, you have school in the morning. Go inside right now."

Hearing I was serious, he pouted but slowly turned and walked towards the gate. He kept looking back at the guys, like they would save him from having to listen to me. He was a curious kid and I knew he wanted to ask questions, but eventually he sighed and let himself out of the gate. "Can I play with your dogs tomorrow?"

Brat. He'd gone around me.

Ben had to clear his throat before his voice came out strong enough to be heard by Forrest. "Sure. The big one is Captain As... You can call him Captain. And the little one is General."

"Awesome! Thank you!" He took off towards the stairs and left me standing amidst three silent men who were each staring at me.

I backed towards the gate, terrified of what was happening. "Well, I'd better go."

"He's ours, isn't he?" Justin stepped towards me. "The

way you're acting and the timeline… Tell me the truth, Violet."

My stomach dropped. "I think I should go…"

Ben marched over to me and cupped the back of my head in one large hand. Forcing my gaze up to his, his teeth were all but bared. "Tell us the truth."

I blinked away the sudden moisture in my eyes and bit my lip hard enough I tasted blood. When Forrest was just a baby, I'd played out scenarios in my head of running into the guys and showing them our son. It'd all been happy and ended in love. Those fantasies had ended years ago, though, and I had no idea what to say or do now the moment arrived.

"He's ours." Mason let out a humorless laugh. "He's six. Unless you went out and had unprotected sex with other men after that night with us, the timing makes sense. We have a son. Is that why you're here? Child support?"

I shook my head hard enough that strands of it got stuck in my face mask. "No! I came here to be close to Margaret and I just love this town. I didn't know you guys would be here!"

"So, you weren't going to tell us that we have a son?" Ben growled out the words as he glared at me.

"I tried!" I pushed away from him and stalked towards the gate. "I tried, dammit. You guys weren't here. I can't do this right now. I need to go up and make sure he goes to sleep."

"You need to go up and read our son to sleep…" Justin ran his hands down his face. "You need to come back down when you're done. You have a lot of explaining to do. You can't just leave us with this."

"I can't. I have Forrest and I need to—"

"You need to come down here and tell us what the fuck is happening. We just found out we have a kid, Violet. The least you can do is talk to us." Mason grimaced. "This is messed up. Does he know about us?"

I closed myself on the other side of the gate and paused for a moment. I met their gazes and shook my head before rushing towards the apartment. Forrest didn't know about them. How would I have explained that to him? *When Mommy was in college, she decided to sow her wild oats with three of the most beautiful men she'd ever seen and that one occasion left her knocked up?* It wasn't exactly a sweet bedtime story.

When I got to the top of the stairs, I stopped and forced myself to take a few deep breaths before facing Forrest. He was perceptive. If I was upset, he'd want to know why. It wasn't just the guys downstairs I didn't have answers for.

Forrest was sitting up in bed, waiting on me with wide eyes. "Who were those men, Mommy?"

I sat next to him and brushed his hair back from his forehead. "They own the house."

"Do you know them?"

"Do you want me to read to you, baby? I need to start now if we're going to do it. It's late and I don't want you acting cranky at school with Ms. Jenny." I grabbed our worn copy of *Harry Potter* and smiled. "Ms. Jenny loves to call me and tell me all about your day, so you'd be smart to always be on your best behavior."

He sighed. "I'm always good, Mom."

I leaned down and kissed his forehead. "You are. No matter what, you're always good, Forrest. You're the best thing in my world, you know that?"

He tapped the book. "I love you, Mommy. Can you

read now, though?"

CHAPTER 4
Violet

I sat next to Forrest after he fell asleep for an amount of time that was probably creepy, considering I was staring at him the whole time. I knew I had to face the guys and doing it while Forrest was asleep was the better choice, but I was putting it off. Forrest had been mine, and mine alone, for six years. The idea of bringing other people into his life who might want to take him, even part time, scared the hell out of me. I was out of my league and so far in over my head.

I'd never thought I'd see the three men waiting on me again. I'd come to Lilyfield to find them after discovering I was pregnant, but they were gone. Without their last names, phone numbers, or any way to contact them, I knew it was hopeless. I'd wanted to find them and give them a chance. I'd wanted to find them and have them tell me they'd lost my number and that was the only reason they hadn't called me after the night we spent together.

I forced myself into the shower to get the face mask off

and then I dressed in the only clothes I wore those days. Leggings and an oversized sweater. I pulled on my boots and turned on the baby monitor I still used to make myself sleep easier with Forrest in a different room to mine. Knowing nothing was going to get easier with waiting, I took my part of the monitor and at the last second, a framed baby picture of Forrest.

Without a single plan or thought in place, I went downstairs and across the yard. The house was lit and I could see through the front windows into a living room where the guys were standing, looking stressed. Even though I wanted to run back to my little apartment and hide away, I made myself walk up the steps to the front door and knock.

Barely a second passed before the door was yanked open and Justin was staring down at me with a focused glare. I passed the framed photo to him and took a deep breath while he dropped his eyes to it.

Ben and Mason appeared behind Justin, each of them staring at the photo of Forrest just as intensely. As I watched, they each studied Forrest with wide eyes.

"He was born on June thirteenth. He was a big baby, ten pounds, and he screamed his head off every night for the first six months of his life. Then, he quietened down and started crawling at big cat speeds. He's always looked like me. He's nothing like me, though. Not really. He's the most charming little boy ever. He's a reader and if he can't read it himself, he wants me to read it to him. Over and over again. He's brilliant and kind. Before we moved here, his last teacher thought he should be moved up at least one grade. He gets bored easily in class and gets himself in trouble. He loves animals, so he'll probably obsess over

General and Captain. He's a really picky eater and can be stubborn. Forrest Channing is the best little boy ever.

"I found out I was pregnant three months after our…time…together. There were no other men after you three. I came back here to find you guys, but you were gone. I met Margaret and she made a big impression, so after living at home with my parents for the past six years, I moved back here to be closer to Margaret. I had no idea you guys were here. I definitely didn't know I would be living in your garage apartment. I didn't plan any of this and I don't exactly know where to go from here."

Justin stepped back from the doorway. "Come in."

I took a shaky breath and moved into the main house, stepping around each of them so I didn't touch them. I was too keyed up to be touched. I was just…scared. I felt like I'd jeopardize my life with Forrest if I didn't play nice.

Justin led me into the living room they'd been pacing through and motioned for me to have a seat on one of the two overstuffed couches. Any other time and I might've appreciated the minimalist decor in the home, but I was too busy trying not to throw up on their hardwood floors.

"Um… Forrest broke his arm when he was three. He was with my Dad and he tried to jump into his arms while he wasn't looking. He landed in the worst way and broke his arm bad enough that he had to have surgery. He has scars from it. He'll need glasses soon. He's happy about it, though. He thinks he'll look like Harry Potter and it'll be cool." I rambled on, trying to fill the silence with whatever facts about my son came to my mind. "He's terrified of needles, but he's literally picked up random snakes he's found on the ground before and carried them around. He kept a pet spider for two months when he turned five. My parents had a cat he became enemies with. If you mention the name Peter, he'll scowl because he really does have a long and awful history with that cat."

Mason sat across from me on the other couch and rested his elbows on his knees. "This all could've been avoided if you hadn't run off."

I frowned, caught off-guard by the change of subject. "I'm sorry?"

"You left while we were at work." He twisted his fingers together. "We wouldn't be here, hearing about our son from you like this, if you hadn't left."

Ben leaned against the doorway behind Mason. "I can't stop thinking about what all we've lost."

Frustration bubbled up inside me, old hurts and shames rearing their heads. "I'm a little confused about why you think this is my fault."

Justin let out a bitter laugh. "Are you serious? You left. We had no clue you were pregnant. If any of us had known you were pregnant, we would've been there. We each had deadbeat fathers; none of us wanted to repeat that history."

I'd tried to find them. They were the ones who never called me. They never made the effort to see me again. They'd left me alone after sleeping with me and I'd been forced to go back to Kansas, knocked up and alone, to be judged harshly by everyone around me, including my parents. I was the idiot who'd left college with one semester left because she hadn't been safe.

"How hard did you look for us?" Mason crossed his arms over his chest and frowned at me. "We were never very far from the Harmony Valley."

"You know what would've avoided all of this? You

three picking up your phones and calling me. Blame me all you want, but this isn't my fault. I tried." I stood up and turned my back on them. "I had to leave because something came up with a friend, but I left a note. I left a note that gave you my number and the reason I had to leave."

Ben grunted. "Bullshit."

I spun back around on them. "I left a note. Don't pretend like you didn't get it just because you're eager to be the victim here. You could've called me. I prayed that one of you would call me. I was twenty-one, raising a kid on my own. I had to go back home to Kansas and listen to every Tom, Dick, and Harry make comments about me being pregnant and all alone. None of it was easy."

"We didn't get a note, Violet." Ben straightened and walked around the couch. "We tried calling your friend, the one you called from our phone, and she told us to fuck off."

My mouth fell open. "You're lying."

"We told you we were coming back after work." He shook his head and looked away. "We tried to find you."

"I thought you lied. People do that. When I had to leave to help my friend, I left a note on the table and I left my number for you guys to call. You never did." I rubbed my temples. "You didn't get the note?"

Mason shook his head. "No. There was no note. We would've called you."

"And told you to get your ass back to us." Justin's growled words left the room in a heavy silence.

CHAPTER 5
Violet

My body erupted in tingles of anticipation as I stared at the three men who'd changed my entire life in one night. They hadn't changed much in six years. If anything, they'd just gotten more handsome. It wasn't fair. Staring up at them made my brain fuzzy.

Ben stood closest to me, his face carefully blank. Six years earlier, his blonde hair had been longer. He'd commented on letting it grow out after getting out of the military. It was neatly buzzed and I noted his beard was almost longer than his hair. The beard was new. As blonde as his hair, it highlighted his tan skin and deep brown eyes. He was bigger. His chest and shoulders seemed wider and he felt taller, even though I knew he probably wasn't. It didn't take much effort for my brain to recall the way his skin had been decorated all over with tattoos, or the way blonde chest hair had been coarse against my lips when I'd kissed my way down his body.

The way he'd grabbed me earlier made me feel like six years hadn't passed. He still touched me like he owned me. My skin heated at that thought and I forced myself to shift my gaze away from him.

Justin walked closer and I swallowed audibly. Bracing his hands on his slim waist, he looked me over and one full eyebrow lifted. "I prefer you without the junk on your face."

I automatically lifted my hands to my face and remembered the mask. Rubbing at my cheeks to hide my embarrassment, I shrugged. "I'm older and a single mom now. Skincare matters. At least, that's what Margaret says. She's seventy and looks forty, so I'm going to believe her."

"A single mom…" Justin shook his head and a few strands of his brown hair fell forward. He shoved the chin-length locks out of his face and narrowed those hazel eyes on me. "It didn't need to be that way."

"It wasn't what I wanted." I wrapped my arms around myself and chewed on my sore lip.

All of my senses were overwhelmed. I could hardly keep up with the way my brain was cataloging changes in the men. Six years was a long time to hold onto a memory, yet I hadn't managed to forget a single thing about them. I still knew the tattoos that covered Justin's arms and while he'd grown a beard, too, I could still see the sharp lines of his jaw. I knew the fullness of his mouth hadn't changed. I knew the exact spot on his chest my lips would rest against if he held me in his strong arms.

"It's hard to not be angry, Violet. I imagined having a kid plenty of times. None of those involved me missing the first part of the kid's life, though. He doesn't know we exist. He doesn't know who we are, at all. We're just strangers." Justin blew out a rough breath and looked down at his boots. "What'd you tell him about his dad?"

"He didn't ask for a long time. He's close with my dad and I don't think he noticed anything different about our family for a while." I looked up as the giant dog came into the room, licking his lips and dripping what I hoped was water all over. He came straight to me and pressed his wet face into my chest.

"Captain Asshole! Go use your towel." Mason stood up and patted the dog's butt. Looking down at my sweater, he winced. "He's usually not *that* friendly."

I looked down and saw that Captain had managed to soak me. Pulling the wet material away from my skin, I shrugged. "He's sweet. Did you call him Captain Asshole?"

Ben grunted. "You'll understand after spending time with him. The little one is General Farts-a-lot. Same explanation."

I pressed my fingertips to my lips to stop a giggle. It didn't feel appropriate, given our tense conversation.

Mason walked out of the living room and came right back with a towel. He came right up to me and pulled the neck of my sweater away from my body so he could drop one end of the towel inside. By the time I reacted, he'd let go of my sweater and had his hand pressed against my chest. He'd pressed my sweater between the two sides of the towel, but the act didn't feel laundry focused when the warmth from his hand seeped through the layers and touched the swells of my breasts.

I took a shaky breath I knew he heard and probably felt. "Thank you."

He flashed a dangerous smile, the same smile that had gotten me out of my shirt all those years earlier. The way his blue eyes crinkled was exactly the same. His deep brown hair was different, the sides shaved and the top longer and curly, and his beard was fuller, but that smile hadn't changed a bit. Just as tall and strong as his best friends, Mason looked down at me and made me feel petite. He'd been able to pick me up and carry me around like I weighed nothing before, but I'd had Forrest and not all of the baby weight had gone away.

That simple reminder that *I* was different, made me want to cry. They'd changed and managed to get sexier. I knew the same wasn't true for me. I couldn't imagine what exactly they saw when they looked at me, but I knew it wasn't the same thing they'd seen the first time around. I was older and I was tired. I felt like the years could be seen on my body.

"I can't make sense of anything right now. Maybe I'm in shock about having a kid, but I'm having a hard time focusing when you're standing right in front of me after all this time." Mason stepped even closer to me. "You being here was the last thing I ever could've expected, but I'm fucking happy to be looking at you."

I tried to look down at my feet but he hooked his finger under my chin and lifted my face. My breath caught when I met his gaze.

"You're not going to sneak out in the middle of the night and leave town, are you?" Mason gripped my waist in his other hand. "I have so many questions and I know we have a lot to talk about, but I need to do something first."

I spoke in a voice barely louder than a whisper. "I'm not leaving."

He nodded. "Good."

I opened my mouth to ask him what he needed to do

but I didn't get the chance to form words before he dipped his head and kissed me. His lips were warm against mine and his beard tickled my face as a swarm of butterflies erupted in my stomach. He shifted his hand to my cheek and then tangled it in my hair before he tugged me closer to his body with his other hand on my waist.

"Mason." Ben's husky voice was firm with disappointment and it was like ice water being thrown over my head.

I tugged away from Mason and moved behind the couch, putting it between us. I ran shaky hands through my hair and licked my lips, which was a mistake because I could taste him. I couldn't look at them. I was embarrassed by my willingness to be kissed like that and concerned about how it made me look.

General walked over to my side and sat, leaning against me with so much weight I stumbled a bit. It didn't phase the giant dog. He looked up at me and his tongue lolled out of the side of his mouth as he panted. I stroked his head, comforted by his presence.

"If you're waiting for me to apologize, it's not going to happen." Mason's voice was soft and when I looked up at him, he shrugged. "We have unfinished business."

CHAPTER 6
Violet

The night we'd shared was never too far from my mind, but standing there in front of them, it might have happened the night before. It was fresh, so raw I could almost hear the sounds of the night through the open cabin windows as they made love to me. It'd been deeper than just sex somehow. By the time morning had come, I'd been halfway in love with the three of them. The connection between us had been unlike anything I'd ever felt and I'd known it was special, not just because it was my first time, but because there was burning chemistry that didn't happen often.

I'd known them for less than twenty-four hours, over six years ago, but I felt such a strong connection to them that it startled me. We'd created a life together, but it was more than that. I'd trusted the men instantly when I met them. I'd been abandoned by friends at the bar in town. We'd driven over three hours to get there, making the trip after hearing about Harmony Valley and all the hot men.

I'd found myself alone, in a town I'd never visited before and knew no one in, and my phone had died pretty much right away.

Justin had spotted me first. The three of them were heading into the bar but when they saw me, they came to my aid. They let me use one of their phones to call my friend, the one who'd left me behind, and then they tried to drive me all the way back to campus. I'd refused, too guilty to make them drive that far just because my friends sucked. I'd asked them to take me to a motel instead, figuring I'd sleep through the night and figure out how to get back to campus the next day. The motel was fully booked, but there were cabins in one of the smaller towns just outside of Lilyfield. They knew the owner and were able to get me set up with a cabin rental for the night.

The cabin had terrified me. It was in the middle of the woods, all by itself, and I'd panicked at the idea of sleeping there alone. I'd been afraid enough that I'd asked the three of them to stay with me for a little while, until I wasn't scared anymore. That led to me asking them to stay the night because I couldn't get over my fear. They'd been perfect gentlemen. Until one touch created a thick tension and the next ignited flames.

I'd given them my virginity that night and they'd given me Forrest. It'd been amazing. They had to report to work the next morning, but they went out and rented the cabin for another night before they left, telling me they wanted me again as soon as they finished work for the day. I'd been smitten, halfway in love, and thrust into a wild sexual desire I needed their help to satiate.

A friend had called right after they left, though. She'd heard I'd been left behind and was on her way to get me.

SUMMER HAZE

Another friend had been dumped the night before and needed me. I hadn't wanted to leave. Not even a bit. I didn't put myself first, or even second, at that point of my life, so I'd ignored my own needs to help a friend. The note I'd left was probably needy, but I wanted to see them again. I *needed* to see them again.

One day had turned into one week, and then into a month, without a word from them. I never told any of my friends what I'd done that night. It felt too special to share with anyone else, even if I believed the guys hadn't cared enough to call me. The night we'd shared became magical in my mind. Despite it hurting when I thought of them writing me off after just one night.

Even when I'd dismissed the idea of ever seeing them again, I still held onto that night like it sparkled with glitter. It'd been so special to me that in all the years since, I hadn't been able to even kiss another man. I'd tried to date, but when it came time to get physical, I just couldn't. There'd been no one before them, and no one after them.

I looked at the three men who'd ruined me for anyone else and a wave of fresh anger struck me. Over half a decade of my life had been scarred by them. I was sure they hadn't thought of me the way I'd thought of them. I had a constant reminder of their existence in Forrest, but even without him, I would've spent too much time daydreaming about them and what might've been.

"I don't want your apology. I don't want anything from you three." I shook my head and moved towards the door. "Maybe you didn't get my note. Maybe you would've called me and we would've found out about Forrest together. That's not what happened, though. Things aren't always pretty. I never should've come back here. You three were clearly fine without knowing any of this. I was fine. Now, it's a mess."

"If you'd known you'd find us here, would you have still moved?" Justin shifted to block my exit.

I hesitated. "I don't know."

"We have a right to know about him and to be a part of his life." Ben growled out at me.

"Of course, you do! I probably would've come, but I would've been better prepared. I would've known what to say and how to say it. I would've prepared myself to see you three again." I lowered my voice. "This is a giant shock to my system. I never thought I'd see you guys again. I don't know how to let go of the hurt right now, and looking at you guys makes me want to cry."

Ben grabbed my hand and spun me into his arms. With my arms pinned between our chests, he held me tight and looked down at me with a frown on his face. "You're here now. We'll figure the rest out."

I swallowed down a lump in my throat. "We will?"

His big hands splayed across my back. "Whether you were ready or not, the cat's out of the bag. We aren't men who are going to walk away from our son. So, yeah, *we'll* figure it out. Together."

I felt a hardness against my stomach and blinked up at him in shock. Of all the things I was expecting, that was the least of them, even after kissing Mason. It was the first time I'd felt an erection in over six years and I was almost scandalized for a moment.

His mouth quirked up on one side and he lifted a shoulder. "I was wrong to stop Mason."

Mason pressed into me from behind. "You really were."

37

My body came alive, throbbing in places that had only ever throbbed for them. I struggled to catch my breath and when Justin joined them around me and gripped my chin, I forgot how to breath completely.

He pulled my face to the side and leaned in closer, until our breaths mingled. "It feels like yesterday you were begging for us to touch you, Vi."

Ben ran his hands down my sides and stopped at my hips. "You said you're a single mom. Single in every sense?"

I nodded at him, even as I told myself to lie and say I wasn't single. I knew I shouldn't be letting them touch me the way they were, but I couldn't stop it. I'd felt so painfully alone and neglected for so long that even just a few touches had me straining for their attention.

"Good. I'd hate to have to dump someone for you." He pulled my mouth to his and kissed me hard, unforgiving in his desire. Shifting his hands to my ass, he lifted me so I had to wrap my legs around him.

Had to might've been a stretch. I was eager. Things that had been dormant for too long were waking up and those things wanted the men around me. All it took for them to understand I was right there with them was me wrapping my arms around Ben's neck. As soon as I did that, the energy in the room shifted.

Mason pulled my hair to one side and used his mouth and even his teeth to tease the sensitive skin at the back of my neck. He pressed himself into my ass and wrapped his arms around me so he could cup each of my breasts. Immediately, he swore and rocked his hips into me harder. "Jesus, Violet These are even better than I remembered."

Ben broke our kiss to look down at my chest. He

pulled the towel off my chest and tossed it behind him. "You grew."

My cheeks heated. "A baby will do that."

Justin cupped my cheek and turned my face back to his so he could kiss me. Lingering, slow kisses that captured my focus and breath. He caught my bottom lip between his and stroked it with his tongue before pulling back and doing it all again.

Mason worked my sweater up and let it bunch while he reached under to cup my bare breasts. His thumbs stroked over my nipples and I gasped into Justin's kiss while bucking my hips into Ben. It'd been so long.

Ben shifted so his stomach was arched away from mine and he could reach the top of my leggings. With the ease of a man who'd done the very act to me before, he reached into my leggings and found me bare. His growl of pleasure was loud, even over my heartbeat thumping in my ears. He cupped my sex and stroked two fingers through my lower lips to gather my wetness.

"Still just as wet as ever for us." Ben's voice was deep and barely restrained. Without preamble, he stroked those two fingers deep into me and I grunted into Justin's kiss. "Fuck. How are you just as tight as the first time?"

Mason dropped one of his hands to my leggings and pressed in next to Ben's hand. "Let me feel."

I tried to relax enough for him to slip his finger in next to Ben's, but I was tight enough it wasn't possible yet. Mason groaned and found my clit instead. Tossing my head back, I let it rest on his shoulder. I bit my lip to stay quiet, but every touch felt like a million jolts of pleasure going through my body.

Justin leaned forward and took my nipple into his

mouth just as Ben curled his fingers in me and made a 'come here' motion. With everything happening all at once, I could barely catch my breath. I opened my mouth and cried out just as another sound filled the room. Static and then a small voice.

"Mommy?"

I gasped and pulled away from them. Yanking my sweater down, I backed towards the front door and stared back at them with wide eyes. "Baby monitor... Have to check on Forrest..."

Ben licked his lips and nodded at me. "Go. We'll see you tomorrow."

I left with the image of the three of them standing there, erections very prominent, watching me with heated gazes like they were far from finished with me. Mason's earlier words filled my head. We had unfinished business.

I made it upstairs and into Forrest's room in record time. Forcing a smile, I knelt beside his bed. "You called me, baby?"

He yawned and stretched his arms out for me. "I'm cold."

I crawled into his bed and pulled him tight against my chest. If he felt my racing heart beating against his cheek, he didn't mention it. I took deep breaths and did my best to calm myself. I couldn't lose my mind every time I was around the men. I had to be stronger than my libido.

I hadn't had much practice trying, though, so it wasn't going to be easy, I worried. Especially when the guys stared at me like I was their favorite meal.

CHAPTER 7
Violet

I dropped Forrest off at school a few minutes early the next morning and then hurried to *Good, Clean Fun*. The front door was locked, but I knocked three times in the special pattern for *Doll's* and Margaret came right away to let me in. She locked the door behind me and then swatted at my butt to rush me into the back.

Doll's smelled like gourmet coffee and pastries every morning, but that morning, there was a little something extra sweet in the air. I looked around, trying to find the source, and spotted Joanie sitting in one of the plush, pink velvet chairs with pink gel all over her hands and chest.

Her cheeks were beet red and she groaned when she saw me watching her. "Don't look at me. I'm an embarrassment."

Margaret snorted. "It's jelly, but not that kind of jelly, Joanie. You're going to be slicker than silk sheets on a slip-n-slide."

I moved closer and sniffed the air around her. "Yum.

Strawberry? It smells delicious."

Both women stared at me with confused expressions on their faces. I chose to ignore it and slipped over to the pastry table. I was starving and something buttery and sweet sounded perfect.

While Margaret helped clean the lube off Joanie, she kept flashing me curious glances. She wasn't one for mincing words, so her hesitation in blurting out whatever she was thinking, made me nervous.

"What? Is there something on my face?" I'd just taken a bite of my chocolate filled croissant when I looked up and made eye contact with a very large dildo. Normally I tried to not look at the toys too much. I blushed easily and just wasn't interested. Looking at that dildo the morning after my run-in with Ben, Justin, and Mason sent heat through my body, only it was to my core and not my cheeks.

"Whoa. The new girl's looking at that PumpMaster 2000 like she's about to tear the plastic open with her teeth. That's new, right?" Brenda Holmes whistled and looked over at Margaret. "Is there something special in that croissant? I'll take three if that's the case."

Yep, there was the blood rushing to my cheeks. Brenda was one of Margaret's two best friends. They were all in their seventies and each as wild as the other. While Margaret had been blessed with the genes of some ancient god which made her age like Jane Fonda, Brenda looked like every grandma in every Christmas story ever written. Short and round, she called herself plump and the description was more accurate than any other I could think of. The third best friend, Coco Jackson, was taller than any other woman I'd ever met and dressed in all black every day. It wasn't a style choice, either. It was because she still fancied herself some sort of secret spy. Where Margaret and Brenda were loud, Coco was silent. She could appear out of nowhere and it was absolutely terrifying.

"There's nothing in the croissants." Joanie sighed as she stood up and walked over to the bathroom. "If I had that kind of power, I'd use it on myself. I'd love to get that look in my eyes over a rubber penis. The PumpMaster 2000 is all I've got to offer myself these days and I just don't get excited about it the way I used to."

"Joanie, babe, you're not even thirty yet. You'd better figure it out." Margaret looked back at me and narrowed her eyes. "Would your moaning over the smell of lube and eye humping the toys have anything to do with your neighbors being home?"

The silence that came over *Doll's* told me they were hungry for the gossip. I'd only lived in Lilyfield for two weeks, but I knew almost everything there was to know because the *Doll's* Club talked. Even with just a few women in the room that early in the day, nothing was sacred. They meant well, though, thankfully.

"I don't know what you're talking about. I didn't moan over the lube. And I was just glancing at the toys. There's nothing different about me." I sat on a pink crushed velvet couch and smiled sweetly. "I did happen to notice my neighbors are back in town, though."

Joanie came out of the bathroom and stripped her shirt off. She pulled on one of Margaret's extra *Good, Clean Fun* shirts and grunted as she sat down next to me. "Be careful if they ask you to sniff the new lube."

Margaret waved Joanie off and her intense gaze focused on me. Her unlined face was a bit too secretive for me to believe it was an accident I'd ended up living in the rental property of the men I'd been looking for six years ago. I'd only ever mentioned their first names to her and only once, the day I'd looked for them. I didn't doubt she could've remembered and set me up, though.

"You got very lucky, getting that rental before anyone else. There's a lot of women in this valley who would love to be that close to those three." She smiled and studied her hot pink nails. "Benjamin McCormick, Justin Jones, and Mason Parker... Those men are beautiful, aren't they?"

Joanie snorted. "Is that a real question?"

I shrugged. "Are they nice? I'm living above their garage, so I probably should've asked before now."

"Super nice." Joanie leaned closer to me. "Great guys with great asses. You can't beat that."

"Are they seeing anyone?" I did my best to look relaxed and unbothered, but I was on the edge of my seat.

"Nope. They stick to themselves most of the time." Studying me, Joanie grinned. "They're always so sweet, though. Ben used to scare people because of how serious he always looks, but he's kind. I bet they'd be good with kids..."

I choked on my croissant and rushed over to grab a glass of fresh lemonade. I guzzled most of a glass and then poured myself more before turning back to face the women who were all watching me a little too closely. I looked everywhere but at them while I drank more, but my eyes kept going to different sex toys. My body reacted to seeing them and I wondered if I'd hit my head the night before.

"They're good men." Coco's face didn't change when I yelped in her face. She'd managed to get right next to me without making a sound. "They hired me when no one else would. Agist pigs make it hard for women like me to work."

Margaret didn't bat an eye at how much Coco had just spoken, but Joanie looked just as floored and I felt. Then Coco's words registered in my horny brain.

"You work for them? Doing what?" I heard the women giggling and looked at where they were looking to see that my hand was idly stroking the PumpMaster 2000's smaller cousin, Thumper 300. I jerked my hand away and glared down at it. "What the hell is wrong with me?"

Coco shrugged at me. "Security."

Margaret clapped her hands and stood as she heard another secret knock on the front door. "I think things are going to get interesting around here."

Joanie shuddered and stood up. "On that note, I think I'll head over to the diner and see how Chase is doing with opening on his own."

I nodded. "Yeah, I'll come with you. It's almost time for me to start, anyway."

Brenda giggled. "Chickens. Don't think leaving will save you from whatever Margaret has planned for you."

"She has plans?" I squeaked and clutched Joanie's arm. "Plans sound scary, right?"

Joanie shuddered again. "Plans sound like I need to move states."

CHAPTER 8
Violet

The *One and Only* had been a faux vintage monstrosity when I'd stepped inside six years earlier. Joanie bought it a couple of years after my visit and she'd turned it into something wholesome and fun. The large glass front let visitors see into the vintage diner and the view was pretty spectacular. The booths were all newly upholstered in a cream color that matched the barstools at the new bar she'd installed. It was classic, instead of the gaudy it had been. She'd even changed out the stained black and white checkerboard floor for a vinyl wood flooring which felt softer underfoot when you had to stand on it for six hours straight.

My favorite thing she'd added was a pie case. I'd only seen them in movies before moving to Lilyfield. The fresh pies she kept inside filled the restaurant with a buttery scent that was renewed every time the case was opened. It was a miracle I hadn't gained twenty pounds since starting, just from how hard I sniffed at the pies.

The only thing I wasn't obsessed about was the uniform. To stick to the vintage theme, the uniform was a pink and cream button-up dress which stopped mid-thigh and white sneakers. The small apron I had to wear over the dress was frilly and made me feel even sillier. Joanie wore the uniform when she worked the floor and she looked amazing. Her long legs were probably one of the reasons she'd chosen the style. It always seemed I was always one gentle breeze away from losing a button and flashing everyone my tits. Or my ass. My curvy figure felt like it tried to eat the dress, but Joanie swore up and down I looked great and she wouldn't let me wear it if I looked bad. I liked her, but I wasn't sure I trusted her that much yet.

That morning, I wasn't in the mood to deal with Jacob Green, an employee at the local military training facility, but I was the only waitress working, since Chase had gone into hiding as soon as he'd seen help arrive. Jacob was very important and impressive, so he'd told me. So important he didn't feel the need to tip, because clearly his presence was present enough. He also ogled my chest and I was half sure I'd caught him praying for my buttons to fail one morning. Every day of the two weeks I'd worked at *The One and Only*, I'd had to deal with him.

He sat at the bar and leaned over it to get his own menu, like he needed one. Joanie had cut the menu down when she took over. It was simple, delicious, and required no fresh glance if you'd been there more than twice. It was like Jacob wanted to feel special, so he made a show of reaching behind the bar. Like he was allowed to when no one else was, but really, no one else was that rude.

I stopped in front of him and forced a smile.

SUMMER HAZE

"Morning, Jacob. Do you want your usual?"

He grinned up at me and spoke to my chest. "I'm craving a little something extra this morning. What do you eat here, honey?"

Joanie had been passing by and she stopped when she heard him. "Her name's Violet. Or you can call her ma'am. You're not an old man who can pull that shit off, Jacob."

I winked at her to show her my thanks and was truly smiling when I looked back at Jacob, but that smile wavered when I saw through the wide-open front glass that Mason, Justin, and Ben were heading into the diner. Without another thought, I dropped into a squat behind the counter and swore at myself in my head as my thighs instantly burned. I wasn't a squat girl.

Jacob leaned over the counter and his eyes lit up like a cartoon, nearly popping out of his head like one, too, when he saw me. "What are you doing?"

I held my dress to my chest so he'd stop looking down it and pretended to look for something on the shelves under the bar. "Just looking for something. I'll take your order in just a second."

"I'll just take my usual. You were right. Smart and beautiful. That's a deadly combination." He kept staring down at me. "How are you liking Lilyfield?"

I yanked out my order pad and scribbled his usual on it. I didn't know how I was going to get it to Aaron, the chef, but I'd done part of my job. I crab walked over a few feet, my thighs on fire the entire time, and glanced up at the small window to the kitchen where we hung the order sheets. Maybe if I hopped up really fast, the guys wouldn't see me? If Joanie came back, I could have her put it on the wheel for Aaron to see.

"Violet?" Jacob said my name too loud and he was following me down the bar, still hanging over it to see me. "I asked how you're liking Lilyfield."

I looked up, ready to strangle him, and watched as Jacob's face was replaced by Mason's. I heard Jacob grunt and start to complain before going silent. Mason's expression was too amused as he leaned his elbows on the bar and rested his chin on his hands. My heart pounded and the burn in my thighs faded slightly as a different burn started between them.

"Whatcha doing?" Mason's grin was painfully handsome and caused my brain to conjure up images of strawberry lube and PumpMaster 2000s.

Since my cover was blown, I cleared my throat and stood up, only stumbling a bit when my sore thighs revolted. I spun around to clip Jacob's order to the wheel for Aaron and when I turned back around, all three men were standing in front of me, their eyes obviously on my ass. I clutched my notepad in my hands. "Just looking for something."

Justin nodded like he believed me. "That's definitely more likely than what we thought. Which was that you saw us coming and ducked down behind this bar to hide."

I forced a laugh. "Of course, not. Why would I hide?"

Ben turned a glare on Jacob who was abnormally silent in his seat. "I can think of one reason a woman in your position might hide."

Joanie came out, spotted the guys, and grinned so wide twin dimples appeared deep in her cheeks. "Well, well, well. Look who's back in town and gracing us with their presence. I would ask what we did to deserve an in-person visit, but I think I already know."

Mason straightened and grinned at me. "I never understood the uniforms before. Good pick, Joanie."

My mouth parted in shock. I couldn't believe his boldness, to openly hint at enjoying my body.

"Mason Parker! Don't harass my employees. Especially Violet. She's everyone's new favorite. I swear, twice as many men from the training facility have been coming in since she started." Joanie grabbed my hand under the bar and squeezed it when she saw I was about to open my mouth and correct her. "Maybe it's even more than twice as many."

I got what she was doing but I was so embarrassed. The guys didn't care about that. She was trying to make them jealous, but I only wanted to cringe and run away.

"Are any of them bothering you, Violet?" Ben's voice was serious as he watched me.

Joanie squeezed my hand harder and then let go and moved away. "Vi can handle a little innocent male attention. Isn't that right, Vi? Now, I need to get to work on the budget. If you need me, just shout."

CHAPTER 9
Violet

Sweat beaded in the center of my back. I wasn't built for lying, in any capacity. Aaron tapped the bell to let me know an order was ready and I jumped at the chance to recover. I grabbed the plate and saw it was Jacob's. I moved and set it down in front of him. Pouring him a cup of coffee, I paused. "Need anything else, Jacob?"

He looked down at the guys and then up at me. His voice was barely above a whisper when he spoke. "Why didn't you tell me you were dating those three?"

I put his coffee down and stared straight at him, not daring to look down the bar at the guys. "I'm not."

He seemed confused, but it didn't seem to matter what I said. "Whatever. Just keep it professional with me from now on."

For the second time in so few minutes, my mouth dropped open. I shook my head, knowing there was nothing I could say that would make me want to throat punch Jacob less. Moving back down the bar, I looked up at the guys and narrowed my eyes at them. "Are you three going to sit and order food?"

Ben shot Jacob another glare. "If he bothers you again, let me know. I'll handle it."

Justin patted Ben's shoulder and nodded to me. "We're taking that booth over there. Can you take a break soon to talk to us about Forrest?"

"Maybe."

He grinned. "I guess we could just ask questions while you take our order and bring us food. That feels a little hectic, though."

"Fine." I rolled my eyes. "Just go sit at your booth. I'll be over in just a second to take your order."

Mason reached across the bar and gently tugged the end of my ponytail. "I really did think this uniform was dumb before you. I think you just unlocked a new kink for me."

I gasped. "You can't just blurt out things like that!"

He laughed easily and shrugged. "What can I say? I like seeing you blush."

I turned away from them while they sat down and met Aaron's eyes through the order window. He was a beautiful dark-skinned man who had an affinity for dangly earrings and gold eyeliner. He was better at makeup than I was and had more style than I could ever hope to have.

His hair was braided and tied up on top of his head but he'd left one braid hanging at his temple. He leaned forward and that braid caught on his eyelashes for a moment before he could push it back. "I heard all of that and I'd be a puddle if I were a woman, girl. Those men are hot and if you get them to keep coming in here, I'll give you my first born."

I covered my face with my order pad and groaned. "Why are all my new friends shameless?"

He laughed and the musical sound filled the diner. "None of us are getting laid, so we're just excited someone might be."

Joanie's voice came from somewhere behind Aaron. "We need to do a sex dance. Like a rain dance, but for sex. What did you do, Vi? Tell us your sex dance secrets."

I spun around and hurried away from the window. I refilled Jacob's coffee and then checked on a few other customers before reaching the booth I was so nervous about.

Justin looked up at me and I could tell by the sparkle in his eyes he'd heard Aaron and Joanie. "I'm going to need to see this sex dance."

Closing my eyes, I groaned and shook my head. "Nope. None of this is happening. I'm going to walk away and come back and it's going to be like you didn't hear any of that."

I did just that but when I got back to their table, Mason was laughing and even Ben looked like he was struggling to keep a straight face. I sighed and sank into the booth next to Ben. He put his arm around my shoulders and pulled me closer, close enough I could smell his woodsy scent. I swooned but tried to hide it.

"You fit in well here." Justin looked me over and slowly shook his head. "Mason's right about the uniform. I want to hug Joanie."

I glanced down at my body and frowned. Were they seeing what I saw? I no longer had the body I'd had at twenty-one, but they were acting like I was the sexiest thing they'd ever seen.

"I don't like that frown, or what I think it means." Justin sat forward and tapped his fingers on the table. "That's a conversation for another time, though. When I tell you how beautiful I find you, I don't want anyone else around to interrupt."

"You're crazy." I muttered and glanced around the diner to make sure everyone was okay. "You wanted to talk about Forrest?"

Ben's arm tightened around me. "He's not crazy. I've been hard since I saw your bare thighs. But that's also for later."

I glanced down at his pants and gulped. The PumpMaster 2000 had nothing on Ben.

"Is Forrest in school?" Justin's grin said he was enjoying my discomfort.

I switched the direction of my brain and nodded. "He's at Lily Elementary. Ms. Jenny is his teacher."

"You said his last school wanted to move him up a grade. You're doing good with him if he's that smart already. None of us were all that bright when we were his age." Mason nodded at Justin and laughed. "I'm pretty sure Justin was still trying to eat his own poop at six."

Justin scowled. "I'm not even going to acknowledge that. Asshole."

"You never finished telling us what you told him about his dad last night." Ben brought the conversation back around but did it while leaning down to sniff my hair. "You still smell like vanilla and raspberries."

I gave up trying not to blush. "Um… About Forrest…" I stuttered. "When he started asking about his dad, I didn't know what to say. For a while, I told him that

I'd tell him about his dad when he was older. But Forrest is a curious kid and doesn't give up. He asked my mom on a day she was feeling especially hateful and she told him I didn't know who his father was because I'd slept around."

"What the fuck?" Justin sat forward. "Why the hell would she do that?"

I shook my head and let out a humorless laugh. "Because she's never forgiven me for getting pregnant. I came back to town without a degree and everyone talked. She and Dad felt like people were judging them for not raising me better. She's a gem, really."

Ben rubbed my arm soothingly and blew out a deep breath. "I'm sorry that happened. You didn't deserve it."

"I just tell myself it's the environment they were raised in. There's no point in crying over it." I shrugged. "After she told Forrest that, I sat him down and had a real conversation about his dad. He knows we lost contact and I've always told him if his dad knew about him, he would've been there."

With a firm nod, Mason agreed. "We would've been there. We weren't ready to let you go back then, Vi."

The butterflies in my stomach were going to be exhausted if they didn't settle down soon. I stared down at my hands and then forced myself to look at them. "Did you really not find a note?"

Ben's voice was stern when he answered. "No. We would've called, Violet. We would've driven to find you as soon as we saw the note."

CHAPTER 10
Violet

I was dragged out of my hopeful feelings by Joanie calling my name. I jumped and turned to see her at the counter, a concerned look on her face. I hurried over to her. "Hey! Sorry. I was just sitting with them for a moment. Did I miss someone?"

She shook her hand. "You're fine, Violet. Forrest's school just called. Jenny couldn't reach you on your cell so she had the secretary call here. They need to see you right away."

My stomach dropped. "Did something happen? Is he okay?"

She grabbed my hand and squeezed it. "It sounded more like a disciplinary thing."

I winced and looked around the diner. "I'm so sorry to have to run out. I'll work an extra shift this weekend to make up for it. I'll come back as soon as I'm finished at the school, too."

"Just go. Don't worry about the diner. I've got this."

She looked at Jacob and scowled. "Let's see how he likes my style of waitressing. I charge an extra dollar every time a man looks at my tits."

I hurried around to get my purse and was intercepted by the guys before I could make it out of the diner. I searched my purse for my car keys and tried to stay calm. "Sorry. I have to run to Forrest's school. Joanie can take care of you, though."

Justin held the door open for me and Mason pointed a key fob across the street to start a giant truck. "We'll drive."

I still couldn't find my keys so I just walked across the street with them. "You don't have to do this. If I can find my keys—"

Ben stopped me next to the back door of the truck. "You're not alone anymore. You don't have to do stuff like this by yourself now. You have us."

Before I could figure out how to climb into my seat, he picked me up and sat me down in the truck. I gasped and had to forced my hands off of his arms once I was settled.

Mason glanced back at me. "Seatbelt."

I fastened the seatbelt in robotic movements as I tried to process what was happening. I was overwhelmed and everything was happening too fast. "You can't tell him that you're his dads, yet."

The three of them remained silent as Mason pulled away from the curb and drove towards Lily Elementary. My panic grew as the silence stretched on. Finally, Ben spoke from his seat in front of me. "We'll follow your lead, Violet, but I'm not sure I understand why we can't tell him. Obviously, we wouldn't do it at school, but what exactly are we waiting on?"

I stammered for a moment and then stopped to take a deep breath and gather my thoughts. "I probably know it doesn't make any sense to you guys, but I need to see you with him. You're his fathers, either way, but this whole thing feels so out of control that I need this one thing. I need to feel like I'm making a healthy choice for him. It's just been the two of us against the world for so long... I'm scared."

Justin reached over and took my hand. "We won't push it right now. None of us can imagine what you're feeling. Just remember we've missed out on so much of his life already and we don't want to miss a moment more. We're going to cherish that little boy, Vi. I promise you, it's a healthy choice."

I swallowed down a ball of emotions. "I don't want you guys to miss anything else, either. He deserves everything he wants in life and I know he wants a dad. Just give me a little time to adjust. You can still be in his life in the meantime."

"As what?" Ben didn't sound happy, but he seemed to accept what I was saying.

"He knows you own the house. We can introduce you as my friends right now. I know it's not perfect, but... Please?" I watched as they each nodded. "Thank you. He's your son and nothing can change that. I just need a little time to adjust."

Mason parked in front of the school and I watched as they opened their doors and got out. Ben opened my door and reached in to unbuckle my seatbelt and pick me up. I squeaked as he did and swatted his arm once I was on the ground. "Stop that. You're going to hurt yourself."

He raised his eyebrows at me. "We're clearly going to

need to work on how you see yourself if you think my picking you up is going to end with me hurt."

Ignoring that, I started towards the school and stopped when I realized they were following me. Turning towards them, I held up my hands and frowned. "What are you doing?"

Mason pointed at the school. "Going to find out what happened with our son."

My face heated and for some reason, my body responded to that statement. I cleared my throat and wrapped my arms around myself. It was chilly in just my uniform, but I barely noticed while standing at the center of their focus. "But we're not telling him, yet."

"That's fine, for now, but you aren't alone in this anymore. He might not know we're his dads, but you do know and we're going to help out in every way we can. Including going in and seeing what's going on." Ben gripped the back of my neck and growled when I shuddered and swayed into him. "If you keep reacting to me touching you like that, we're never going to make it in because I'm going to drag you back to the truck and fuck you senseless. Understand?"

I forced myself away from them and took a deep, shaky breath. "You can't say things like that. We haven't seen each other in almost seven years. It's not like you can just pick up where you left off."

Mason smirked. "Does it feel like we haven't seen each other in that long to you? Because to me, it feels like you were just spread out beneath us yesterday. If you knew how many times I've thought about you since that night, you'd understand why it's so easy for us to pick up where we left off."

A bell rang and startled me out of whatever I was going to say. I spun around and found that through the glass doors, I could see students moving about. The older grades were switching classes. Looking back at the guys, I found each of them smiling back at me. I barely resisted the urge to check my face for crumbs. "What?"

Ben shook his head and nodded towards the doors. "You're cute when you're flustered. Now, come on. Let's go see what's up with our son."

My heart fluttered and I pressed my hand over it, like that would calm the silly thing down.

Justin took my other hand and pressed it over his own racing heart. "We're all feeling it, Vi. We have a son together. I don't know if I'll ever hear that and not feel a rush of adrenaline. I know it hasn't been what we would've wanted up until this point, but that all changes now."

CHAPTER 11
Justin

Violet walked into the school ahead of us and it took every ounce of my control to not stare at her full ass. We were walking into a school and it made me feel like a creep thinking anything remotely sexual. Still, her long legs and juicy thighs disappearing under the hem of that short dress made it hard not to stare. She'd always been beautiful, but she'd somehow gotten even more so than the recurring dream version of her in my head. Her body was curvier now, her breasts fuller. She'd gotten sexier since our night together and it was wreaking havoc on my thoughts.

I nearly walked over her as she stopped at the front desk, where an eagle-eyed older woman stared at us. I smiled and nodded at her, suddenly overcome with a worry that I'd never felt before. Did we look like dads? I knew the three of us didn't exactly look like teddy bears, but at least Mason and I smiled often enough to ease people's concerns. Would the woman sitting at the desk even trust us to be inside the school?

"Hi. I'm Violet Channing. I was called about my son, Forrest." Violet fidgeted, clearly worried.

I could remember my mom being called to the school to hear a laundry list of shit I'd done that day. She'd always ripped me a new one for disturbing her. As I studied Violet's profile, I tried to imagine her snapping at Forrest and couldn't.

"Oh, yes. I'll page Ms. Jenny and have her come down to meet with you. Forrest is sitting outside the principal's office if you'd like to wait with him." The woman pointed us in the right direction and I had to make myself walk slowly behind Violet. All I wanted to do was run to Forrest and look at him.

The moment Violet spotted him, her shoulders dropped a solid two inches. She'd been worried. She hurried over to him and knelt in front of him, putting strain on the bottom of the dress that was hard to look away from. "Are you okay?"

I knew Ben and Mason were feeling the same thing I was. Our parents never would've checked on us first. Seeing Violet drop down to Forrest's level and ask if he was okay made a lump form in my throat. She was a good mom. If things had to happen the way they did, at least Forrest had had her for the beginning of his life.

Forrest shrugged. "I'm okay, Mom."

She pushed his hair behind his ears and cupped his cheeks. "You don't have to say you're okay if you don't feel that way, baby. Tell me what you're really feeling."

I watched as the boy did something most adults couldn't. He took a deep breath and thought for a moment before answering his mother. "I'm mad. I'm scared, too."

Violet nodded. "Thank you for telling me that. What are you scared of?"

"That you're going to be mad at me." He looked up and spotted us for the first time. That spoke to how thoroughly he'd been focused on his mom, because we weren't easy to miss. He looked like he had questions but Violet regained his focus when she spoke.

"You know being mad is a completely normal thing. Even if I did get mad, it would never last very long and we would always talk about it afterwards. Just like when you got mad at me last week, right?" She waited for him to nod and then pressed on. "I love you through all of my emotions. Wanna tell me what you're mad about?"

Before he could answer, a woman I recognized from around town walked up to us. She looked confused at seeing the three of us there with Violet, but everyone was going to have to get used to it. We weren't going anywhere.

Violet stood up and adjusted her uniform before smiling tightly at Jenny. "Hi, Ms. Jenny. I got here as fast as I could."

"I'm sorry to have to take you away from work, but this was an urgent matter. Principal Boyd is ready for us, so if you'll just follow me. You, too, Forrest."

Violet noticed the way the teacher was eyeing us suspiciously and tugged at the bottom of her uniform again. "I'm not sure if you know my friends. Ben, Mason, and Justin will be joining us today. I'm living over their garage and they're helping out."

I didn't like being called her friend, but I understood she couldn't be honest with the teacher. I nodded at the other woman again and amped up the charm in my smile.

"I've seen you around town. We don't get out much, though, so we haven't officially met. It's nice to meet you, Jenny."

The blush on her cheeks made me take a step closer to Violet. Violet, however, took a step away from us and frowned as she watched Jenny smile at us. Violet didn't seem to like the teacher giving us that flirty smile. Was it possible that our little flower was jealous?

I met Ben's eyes and I could tell by the way he smirked he thought she was, too. Mason, never one to shy away from saying whatever he wanted, easily reached down and took Violet's hand. "We're very, very good friends."

Violet's face went bright red but she didn't snatch her hand away. Not until it was clear Jenny got the message. I couldn't wait to have that conversation at a later date. Even though she'd surely deny it, Violet had a jealous streak.

Jenny clasped her hands together and nodded. "If you'd all follow me."

We did just that and ended up cramped inside Adam Boyd's office. Boyd had been involved with the training facility while we went through our paces there and he'd been power hungry then. I could only imagine how much he liked lording it over all the children and teachers under his command.

Violet sat in one of the two chairs in front of Boyd's desk and I watched his eyes flick down at her thighs. Moving to stand behind her, I put a hand on her shoulder and glared at Boyd. He'd be smart to keep his eyes to himself.

After clearing his throat, Boyd started a talk that sounded too rehearsed. "While Ms. Jenny is going to be in charge of this conversation, I'm here to be support for both of you. Getting called in here is never easy, whether you're the student, or the parent. I'm here to make this as smooth as possible. Ms. Jenny, you can go ahead."

I wanted to punch the man. I'd been called into enough principal's offices in my day to know he would back his teacher until his dying breath. He wasn't support for Violet or Forrest.

"First, let me say that Forrest is an exceptionally bright young man. He's reading on a third-grade level and will be even higher than that in no time, I'm sure. It's only been a couple of weeks with him in my class, but he's brightened the place up. He's friendly and lovely to everyone. Which is why today was such a surprise." Jenny took a breath and looked at Forrest. "During our morning read-a-loud, Forrest pushed another student out of his chair. It was shocking, to say the least. We have a zero-tolerance policy for any kind of physical violence at this school. Because of that, Forrest can't come back to class today. He can return tomorrow, but he'll need to be prepared to apologize to the other child."

Violet looked at Forrest. "Can you tell me what happened?"

Boyd cleared his throat again. "No matter what, he's being suspended for the day, Ms. Channing."

Ben grunted. "I'd hope that part of the support you offer is listening, Boyd."

The older man started straightening his desk and stammered. "Of course. Go ahead."

Violet glanced up at Ben and smiled before looking back at our son. "Tell me what happened, Forrest. Please."

"Jake was being mean to Sophie. He kept pulling her

hair when Ms. Jenny wasn't looking. I told him to stop but he didn't. Sophie got sad and he called her a crybaby. He tried to pull her hair again so I pushed him to make him stop. I didn't mean to push him out of his chair. I just wanted him to leave Sophie alone." He blinked up at me and his little frown wobbled. "I'm not going to get to play with your dogs today, am I?"

I dropped to my knees in front of him and rested my hand on his tiny shoulder. "As long as your mom says it's okay, you can play with the dogs every day. It sounds to me like Jake was being a bully and you tried to stop him. That's pretty cool, dude."

Violet put her hand on my shoulder and gave me a pointed look before smiling at Forrest. "It is really cool you tried to stop a bully, Forrest. Next time, maybe try to tell Ms. Jenny first, though. I'm proud of you for standing up for Sophie. Let's try to do it without touching anyone else next time. Okay?"

Forrest scuffed his feet on the linoleum and nodded. "Okay, Mommy."

"Did you know Jake was bullying Sophie?" Violet had turned back to Ms. Jenny, who looked horrified.

"No. Sophie didn't say anything. After Forrest pushed Jake, I sent him straight here." She looked at Forrest. "I'm really sorry I didn't stop to ask you what happened, Forrest. Your Mom's right. We aren't supposed to touch other people without permission, but it was kind of you to stand up for Sophie."

"So, the suspension...?" Ben looked at Boyd with raised eyebrows.

"It stands. Zero-tolerance is zero-tolerance." Boyd clasped his hands together on top of his desk and nodded, dismissing us. "If anything like this should arise again, Ms. Channing, I recommend being a little firmer with the boy. He's bigger than the other kids his age. He could hurt someone. Next time, I'll make it a week-long suspension. You set him straight at home or I won't let him back. This is a good school."

I stood up, ready to rip his head off, but Violet beat me to it. Plus, she did it with a sweet smile on her face. "Thank you for the parenting advice, Principal Boyd, but you'll have to forgive me if I don't subscribe to the firmer action I can only imagine you're talking about. I prefer to raise a son who stands up to bullies instead of becoming one. You have a good day, though."

Violet took Forrest's hand and led him out of the office. Jenny followed after us and quickly got ahead of Violet, where she gently stopped her. "I'm so sorry. He's not normally *that* harsh. If I'd known the whole situation, I wouldn't have gotten him involved at all. I'll be sure to have a talk with Jake and I don't expect Forrest to apologize in the morning."

"Thank you. Forrest will apologize for pushing Jake, though. Sometimes we make mistakes, like pushing someone out of their chair, and even if our reasoning was good, the action was still wrong." Violet smiled down at Forrest. "Don't worry about this kid, though, because he's getting ice cream and pie for stopping a bully from making someone cry."

Forrest's eyes widened and he stared up at his mom in awe. "Really?"

Jenny held her hand out to Forrest. "Still friends, Forrest?"

He shook her hand and grinned. That smile looked so

much like his mother's that it took my breath away. "Still friends, Ms. Jenny."

We said goodbye and made our way outside, where Forrest immediately turned to us and let the questions fly.

"Why are you here? Who are you? Are you my mom's boyfriends? Can Moms have boyfriends? Is that your truck? Where'd you get your dogs?"

Mason laughed easily and held out his hand to count out his answers. "We're here because we wanted to make sure you and your mom were okay. We're your neighbors and your mom's friends. I know we'd like to be your mom's boyfriends, but that's up to her. Moms can definitely have boyfriends. That is my truck. And our dogs came from my sister, Jenna. She thought we needed pets to take care of. So, she gave us a giant dog who drools everywhere and knocks people over all the time and a tiny dog who farts at least a hundred times a day."

Forrest laughed hard enough he stumbled. Mason caught him and they both laughed like they'd never heard anything funnier. I caught the smile on Violet's face as she watched them, her hand pressed over her heart again.

I inched closer and pressed my hand to the small of her back. "You didn't freak out over the boyfriend comment. I'm taking that as a good sign for us."

She rolled her eyes. "Consider it a temporary lapse in judgment."

CHAPTER 12
Violet

I looked at my phone and read the text that had just come in from Margaret. She'd called an emergency meeting at *Doll's*. I'd never seen her do that before, so I felt a sense of urgency to get there for her. I looked over at where Forrest was playing in the yard with the dogs and frowned.

"What is it?" Ben moved closer and tipped my chin up so I would meet his gaze.

"Margaret needs me to come over…"

"We can hang out with Forrest while you're gone." He saw my hesitant expression and cupped my cheek. That gesture melted me every time and I felt like he knew it. "Go see Margaret. We want to get to know Forrest better and he's having so much fun with the dogs. We won't let anything happen to him, Vi."

I knew that. Watching them with Forrest that afternoon, I'd seen how good they were to Forrest right away. Even when they were in Principal Boyd's office, they'd made me feel like I wasn't alone for a change. They had my back. More importantly, they had Forrest's back.

"We're not going to do anything or say anything to jeopardize our time with both of you." He smiled and nodded. "Yeah, I said both of you. After the way we've been throwing ourselves at you, I'm a little surprised you seem surprised by that statement."

Forrest yelled for me and when I looked, he was proudly walking Captain around on his leash. "Captain is so cool, Mom!"

I couldn't help the smile that stretched my lips. "Yeah, he is. Now I know you can walk him, I think I'll sleep in on those cold mornings this winter and let you walk the dogs."

"Okay!" He walked Captain back to Justin and then took General. General immediately took off at a sprint and dragged Forrest along behind him. Back and forth across the yard they went, neither of them stopping until Mason stepped in and scooped up the little dog. Forrest flopped onto the ground. "Whoa."

I laughed and bit my lip before looking up at Ben. "Okay. I won't be gone long, though. And I can grab dinner while I'm out, so you don't have to feed him."

"We'll take care of it, Vi. Take as long as you need." He pressed a kiss to my forehead like he'd been doing the same thing every day since the night we met. "Don't take *too* long, though, because I like the view when you're around."

I groaned. "You don't have to butter me up."

"One of these days, Violet… One of these days." He patted my ass and nodded to Forrest. "Anything we need to know? Allergies? Fears?"

"He'll tell you everything he will or won't eat, so that'll be clear for you. He's not allergic to any foods. He is allergic to penicillin and wasps. And as long as you don't try to give him a shot, you don't have to worry about his fears." I walked over to the fence and called Forrest. "I'm going to go meet with Ms. Margaret. The guys volunteered to hang out with you while I'm gone. How does that sound?"

He threw his fists in the air. "Boys only night!"

I frowned. "It's too early for you to be that excited about getting rid of me."

He reached over the picket fence and gave me the best hug he could from that angle. "I still love you, Mom. Mason said he has racing games we can play, though."

"Fine, fine. I love you, too, Forrest. Be kind and respectful, okay?" I caught his little face in my hands and leaned over to blow a raspberry on his forehead. "I'll be back."

He groaned and wiped his forehead before running back to play with the dogs. He started telling an animated story to both Justin and Mason, instantly forgetting about me leaving.

I turned to Ben and smiled. "I don't know how you'll manage to tear him from me when he's so clearly clinging on for dear life."

He laughed. "Sorry, but it's boys' night. No girls allowed."

I grunted and headed towards the apartment to grab my purse. "I'll be sure to remember that."

When I got to *Doll's*, the back room was full and the energy chaotic. Margaret stood with her back to the door, facing the room, and her arms were windmilling as she ranted. "And then he said this store is a waste of space and would be better for the community if it was used as more training space."

Joanie waved me over and I squeezed onto the couch between her and another woman I didn't recognize. I smiled at her and thanked her for making room for me.

"Leaving someone standing during one of Margaret's rants against Mayor Stevens would be criminal." The pretty blonde held out her hand and shook mine. "Billie. You must be Violet."

I let out a surprised laugh. "This really is such a small town."

"It is. You can't miss a new face." Billie nodded over at Joanie. "Plus, Joanie might've mentioned something about Violet heading our way."

Margaret raised her voice over us and we had no choice but to focus on her. Brenda and Coco were standing behind her like good soldiers. "I'm done being pushed around by that man. I swear he's had a stick up his ass since I turned him down all those years ago. He's twenty years younger than me! I was doing him a favor!"

Brenda crossed her arms over her ample chest and shook her head. "He has no idea who he's messing with."

"He had the nerve to say my soaps and candles are giving everyone headaches. That's such bullshit. If anyone around here has a headache, it's from listening to him drone on and on." Margaret seethed and planted her hands on her hips. "Honestly, I should've decked him."

Eve Michaels shrugged. "I'm sure Grandpa wouldn't have minded."

"How is your grandpa doing, honey? I didn't see him around this morning." Brenda left her warrior pose for a moment to check on Eve. I'd learned she'd moved back to town not too long ago to help take care of her grandpa, who happened to be the Harmony Valley sheriff. He also happened to be pretty old and in failing health.

"He's okay." Eve's voice sounded strained. "As cantankerous as ever. Dr. Dukes said the new medicine should have him up and running soon, but so far, all it's got running is his mouth. He told me I was getting old this morning."

We all hissed in understanding. There were some things you just didn't say to a woman. Brenda clutched her pearls and her blue-coated eyelids disappeared as her eyes widened comically. "Oh, no. Hank knows better!"

Lizzie Jackson, Coco's niece, brought the conversation back around to Margaret. "If Sheriff Michaels won't be on hand to approve of you decking Mayor Stevens, what's your next move?"

Margaret's face changed into something more conniving. "Well, that's what I was getting to. After arguing for a while, Mayor Stevens and I decided it's time to settle who's better in this town. Me or him? The fantastic women or the bozo men?"

I leaned forward and tilted my head as I tried to make sense of her words. "Like a battle of the sexes?"

She nodded and rubbed her hands together. "Exactly. We're going to put that horse's ass in his place, for once and for all."

CHAPTER 13
Violet

The meeting ended and most of the women filed out, their minds probably as full of Harmony Valley strangeness as mine. When I didn't leave right away, Joanie and Margaret closed in on me and we shared a couple of cupcakes while I opened up to them. I had a feeling Margaret already knew, but I needed advice.

"I'm sorry, but did you just say that they're Forrest's dads?" Joanie put her half of the cupcake down and shook her head. "How is that possible?"

I told them a short version of the story and watched Joanie's face as she slowly put together the same thing that I'd put together. Margaret had a hand in my reunion with the guys. We both looked at Margaret and she pretended to be inspecting her perfect nails.

"I don't know why you're looking at me." She looked up at me and smiled. "So, it sounds like they want you. Are you going to sleep with them?"

I gasped and both women laughed. Joanie patted my

knee and pushed the rest of her cupcake towards me. "You need this. And an orgasm from a real human."

"I can't just sleep with them. It's all too connected, don't you think? I live in their guest apartment. They're going to be involved in Forrest's life. I don't want to mess things up."

Margaret stood up and grabbed one of the gift bags which sat on a shelf above a rack of lingerie. "Stop thinking so much and just let it happen. You want them. So have them. I'll give you the same thing I give every Harmony Valley woman who's starting a budding sexual relationship. It's a bag of tricks to help you and your fellas know exactly what you want. Though, I don't think the three of them will have any trouble."

I clutched the bag to my stomach and pressed my hand to my warm face. "Thank you. I don't think I'll do it, though."

Joanie stood up and stretched. "If you don't, you're an idiot. Those men are beautiful. You have a chance to get what you wanted all those years ago."

"Take what you want, Violet. If you don't, someone else might." Margaret stood up and pulled me to my feet. "I wouldn't lie to you. They're good men. Smart and protective, too."

"And that's supposed to be enough for me to chance ruining everything?"

Joanie snorted. "The only thing you're ruining is your sex life if you don't take a chance. Have a little faith. Maybe something good will come of this."

I walked with them to the front of the store and took a deep breath of the early fall air once we were on the sidewalk. "They're watching Forrest right now. Is it crazy I wasn't worried at all about leaving him with them?"

Margaret wrapped her arm around my shoulder. "No. They're his dads. You can feel the truth about those men. Just like you could six years ago. They're good men."

I leaned into her and sighed. "It isn't easy to let go of all the hurt feelings I've harbored since not hearing from them."

Joanie looked down the street towards the diner and groaned. "I have to run. Chase and his brother Charlie were supposed to be running things while I stepped out but judging by the crowd outside the diner, I'm guessing they managed to fuck something up. I'll see you guys later."

I waved goodbye and wished her luck. Margaret grinned at her with a twinkle in her eye. "Could just be a crowd of women gathering to stare at the new eye candy you've got helping out."

Joanie's eyes narrowed as she backed away. "Stay out of it, Margaret. Keep your focus on Violet."

"Hey!" I pouted. "I don't want anyone's focus right now."

After Joanie hurried away, Margaret looked down at me with that same twinkle in her eye. "You hurry up and get home to your boys."

"*Boy.* Singular boy." I unlocked my car and held the door open, hesitating before getting in. "Did you know they were here all along?"

She rested her hand on top of mine and shook her head. "When you mentioned their names that day you showed up, I didn't recognize them. I wrote them down in my journal, the same way I write down everything, but I immediately forgot those three names. I think I assumed they were soldiers who were only in town for training. I like to go through my old journals every so often, though. I like to see how my feelings have changed for certain people around here. Six years ago, I thought Mayor Stevens was a hapless fool, but now? Now, I think he's a pompous ass who could fall off a cliff. When I saw your guys' names, I happened to recognize them."

"And you thought you'd make plans for me?"

She made a motion like she was zipping her lips. "I don't know what you're talking about. Get home to them now. I'm sure they're missing you."

I grunted at her. "You're lucky they didn't take one look at me and bolt."

"If you think that was even remotely possible, we need to work on your self-confidence, girl. You're a stunner with a beautiful personality. Those men are probably tripping over themselves to convince you to give them a chance."

I slid into my car. "You're crazier than I thought."

She pretended to tip a hat at me. "Thank you. I'll see you tomorrow. Use that bag of tricks. If you're not walking with a visible limp tomorrow, I'm going to be disappointed."

"Oh, my god! You can't just say things like that, Margaret!" I laughed even as my face burned. "You're wild, you know that?"

She winked at me. "How do you think I managed to stay single for so long? No man can handle me."

She shut my car door and sauntered off, heading straight towards Mayor Stevens, where he was coming out of Barry's Barbershop. The man was as bald as a newborn, but everyone whispered he had Barry shave and shine his head weekly. It was rumored that in the summer he had to drench his head with sunblock and a matting powder to keep from burning and blinding everyone with the shine.

I was tempted to stick around and watch their interaction, but Margaret turned and made a *shoo*ing motion at me. Waving at her, I gave up on getting information to share with the other Dolls and drove home. I parked in the garage and gathered my things to carry upstairs but before I could get to the stairs, I heard Forrest's laughter. Not wanting to miss out on him having a fun time, I went around to the main house and searched for him.

To my surprise, he was inside with Justin, Mason, and Ben, and his laughter had carried through the open windows of the living room. He was laughing louder than I'd ever heard him laugh and after letting myself into the front yard and walking towards the front of the house, I could see him in the living room with the guys, playing a board game. For a moment, I felt a stirring of jealousy. He was *mine*. I didn't know what it meant to share him. I wasn't sure I wanted to anymore.

Then Forrest looked up at the guys and the smile on his face was so excited, I was immediately ashamed for wanting to take him away from the guys. He was already crazy about them. I didn't know if he could feel the thing that connected them to each other, but I'd never seen him connect with another person so quickly.

I felt a deep yearning to be a part of their little group so I knocked on the front door and waiting impatiently for them to let me in. It was Forrest who pulled the door open for me and he leapt into my arms when he had enough room to bolt out of the house. I stumbled back and nearly lost my balance. "Whoa! You're getting so tall and strong! Have you ever considered football?"

He hopped down and grabbed my hand to drag me inside with him, straight back to the living room I'd stood in and been kissed not too long before. As soon as we were in the room, he dropped my hand and settled on the couch with Justin and Ben again. "We're playing a train game! You have to build your trains and connect them from city to city!"

General and Captain both came over to greet me so I bent and petted them while smiling. General jumped, trying to get as high as Captain, but he was just too small. I picked him up and walked farther into the room. "You four look like you're having a great time."

Mason held up one of the tiny trains. "How could we not be having fun? We're all train conductors, making our way across the country. Isn't that every kid's dream?"

I snorted. "My dream as a kid was to get a puppy and live outside with it."

Forrest threw his head back and cackled. "You wanted to live outside?! You can't live outside, Mommy. Where would you put all your books?"

"I didn't have as many back then. Grandma and Grandpa didn't like it when I bought books, so I used the library." I saw the question on his face and went ahead with an answer. "The bookstore was in another town and it was expensive. They thought it was a waste of money. As soon as I was old enough to make my own money, though, they couldn't stop me. That's when I started collecting all the books you love so much now. If we lived outside, I'd have to make sure we had a house for our books."

"A house for the books but not for us? You're silly, Mom!" He looked up at Ben and smiled shyly. "Isn't she?"

Ben ruffled his hair and looked up at me. "She's a little silly, but she's a lot pretty."

I rolled my eyes and was opening my mouth to say something sassy back at him but I felt a tug on the bag in my hands. I looked down to see General with his mouth on the gift bag Margaret had given me. In the split second it took me to remember what was in the bag, it was too late. General closed his giant mouth around the bag and pulled harder, ripped the bag away from its twine handles and the next thing I knew, he shook his head happily and sent an impressive collection of sex toys flying in every direction.

CHAPTER 14
Ben

It took me a few seconds to realize what I was looking at. A rainbow of sex toys had just exploded in the living room. General Asshole panted happily and tossed the now empty bag in the air. I made eye contact with a hot pink cock ring and raised my eyebrows.

Violet gasped and when I looked up at her I couldn't help smiling. She was bright red and her mouth was opening and closing like she had something to say, but no words came out. She was staring at a rainbow dildo that sat at her feet, upright. It was standing tall and proud, staring up at her. She finally squeaked and ducked down to grab the dildo. It was suctioned to the hardwood floor, however, and it took her a few good tugs to get it up.

Mason leaned forward and picked up a glittery butt plug. "Wow."

"You dropped your lipstick, Mom." Forrest picked up a bright red bullet and lifted it towards his mouth like he was going to put lipstick on.

I grabbed the bullet and shoved it into my pocket. "Sorry, buddy, if you want to wear lipstick, you're going to have to wait another few years."

Violet finally found her voice. "Can I have a glass of water? Can everyone go together to get it for me?"

Justin sounded like he was straining to contain a laugh. "Yep. Let's go, little man. You can push the ice button."

"The ice button? You mean to make the ice come out of the door? That's not special. Grandma has one of those on her fridge, too." Forrest still stood and followed Justin and Mason.

"I bet your Grandma's ice maker doesn't make ice like ours. Wait until you see it." Mason slipped the butt plug into his pocket and wagged his brows at Violet. "Just in case."

She covered her face with her hands and grunted. She was still holding the rainbow dildo in her hand and she'd poked herself in the eye with it. "Can this get any more embarrassing?"

I made sure the guys were out of the room with Forrest and then I stood and tugged a surprised Violet into my body. She dropped her hands from her face and the dildo fell before she rested her hands on my chest. I searched her bright green eyes and ran one of my hands through her long auburn hair. She was fucking beautiful. She'd only gotten prettier since the night we'd met. Her hair was longer and her curves were fuller, but her heart shaped face and full mouth were the same.

"Who'd you get all those toys for?" I watched as her eyes widened and tightened my hand in her hair. I liked it longer, I decided.

Violet licked her lips and took a shaky breath, her

pupils dilating as she stared up at me. "What?"

I tightened my arm around her waist and lowered my voice to a growl. "Who'd you buy all these toys for?"

She shuddered in my arms and let out a breathy sigh before she seemed to remember herself. "That's none of your business."

She was pouring gasoline on a fire. I walked her back until she was pinned between me and the wall. "You don't actually believe that, do you?"

"It... It isn't."

I ran my hand down to her ass and squeezed the fullness of the bottom curve. My fingers dipped lower and I could feel her heat through the leggings. "It isn't my business?"

She tipped her head back when I tightened my hold on her hair and a small moan escaped her pouty mouth. "It's not."

My dick was harder than I could ever remember it being. I ground it against her stomach and dug my fingers into the crack of her ass. "The hell it's not. Do I need to remind you why it's my business?"

She let her head thump against the wall. "Ben..."

I dropped my mouth to her neck to taste her sweet skin. I spoke against her ear and ran my fingertips up and down her ass, loving the way she shuddered when my fingers grazed her asshole. "In case it slipped your mind, I took your virginity, Vi. I fucked you first. I broke your hymen and stretched you out before anyone else. That was me. I came deep inside you before anyone. You're more my business than anyone has ever been. So, tell me. Who'd you buy these toys for?"

Her chest brushed against mine with every ragged

breath she took. "I didn't buy them. They were a gift. To use with you guys."

I all but purred at her admission. "Do you know why you're supposed to use them with us?"

She met my gaze and looked pained as she shook her head. Biting her lip, she shifted her hips to press into me and then arched them away from me. She couldn't decide what she wanted. She didn't answer my question, but her eyes were pleading as she continued the back and forth with her hips.

"It's because you're still ours. After all this time, you still belong with us." I heard the guys coming back and stepped away from Violet. "*You're* my business, Violet."

She let out a quiet whine and reached for me, but I shook my head and nodded back at where Forrest was trailing in after Justin and Mason. Swallowing, she straightened and then dropped to her knees in front of me. I nearly choked until she looked up at me with a handful of sex toys. "Help me!"

Laughing, I joined her in gathering the rest of the gifts. By the time Forrest was carefully putting a glass of water down for his mom, we'd picked up every sex toy we could see. I watched with tears of laughter as Violet spotted a vase on a bookshelf and hurriedly stuffed the toys into it.

Mason gasped. "That was my grandma!"

Violet's face paled and she looked back and forth between Mason and the vase, her hand awkwardly hanging in the air over the vase. She slowly lowered her hand towards the opening with a wince all over her face. "Should I get the toys out…?"

Throwing his head back and laughing, Mason didn't see the cock ring Violet threw at him. It hit him in the throat and bounced off, just to fall into the glass of water.

Forrest shrugged happily. "I'll go get more ice! Mom, their fridge makes square ice!"

"To be clear, this isn't anyone's grandma, right?" Violet shuddered in horror. "If it is, I think I have to leave and never come back here."

Mason grinned at her while rubbing his throat. "No, I didn't store my grandma in an open vase. Also, nice aim."

She rubbed her temples and then rested her hands over her chest. "You scared me so bad. I really thought I was about to be haunted by one supremely offended grandma. I'd definitely haunt someone if they dropped a rainbow dil-*pickle*. If someone dropped a dill pickle on me? So mad."

Forrest ran back into the room with a square block of ice in his hands. "Here you go, Mom!"

Violet took the ice and juggled it between her hands as she bent forward and pressed a kiss to his head. "Thanks, baby."

Justin handed her the glass, sans the cock ring, and watched her with humor-filled eyes. "You definitely make life more colorful, Vi."

She grunted and drained the glass of water before handing it back to him. "On that note, I think it's time to go home and start making supper."

"But, Mom!"

"No buts, mister. You got to spend all day over here. You can see everyone again tomorrow." Violet looked up at Justin. "What time should I come over to walk General and Captain in the morning?"

The three of us shook our heads in unison. I wasn't sure how she'd take the next bit of news, so I just spit it out. "We don't need you to walk the dogs anymore."

She frowned. "Why not?"

"Because you're the mother of our—" I cut myself off. "Because General and Captain can be a lot and we'd feel better if you weren't out, walking around on your own."

She planted her hands on her hips. "Then give me another job. I'm not staying for free."

Mason shrugged. "You are."

She shook her head hard enough to send her hair flying around. "I'll walk the dogs then. I'm not helpless."

"If you want to join me on my morning walk with the dogs at seven each morning, I won't stop you." Justin pulled two walkie-talkies out of his pocket and handed one to Forrest. "This way, you can call us if you need us. Your mom was right about you being too young to be the man of the house right now. We'll take that job, if you want."

Forrest took the walkie-talkie and jumped up and down. "I've always wanted a walkie-talkie!"

Violet sighed. "I hope you know what you just started."

At least she seemed distracted from the dog walking. I watched as she turned towards our front door and cast one last look back at us. With the sunlight coming in from behind her, she looked like an angel. She glowed, just like the night we'd met. She'd been standing under a neon bar sign and she'd looked like a goddess.

We'd all fallen for her instantly back then. I had a feeling time had done nothing to dull that reaction in us. There was just something about Violet.

CHAPTER 15
Violet

"You'd better be in bed with your teeth brushed, kid!" I finished putting away our left-overs and washed my hands. "If you're not, you're going to be surprised when I make Voldemort look sweet and innocent!"

I heard giggling and when I made it to Forrest's bedroom, I saw he was under his blanket with a flashlight. I stood in the doorway to see what he was doing and felt my heart melt when I heard a static crackle and my son's urgent whispering.

"Mom's coming! I have to go!"

"Alright, Forrest. Listen to your Mom." Justin's voice was slightly robotic through the walkie-talkie. "Give her a kiss on the cheek for me."

Forrest giggled. "Mommy never lets boys kiss her. My friend, Bonnie, says her mom is always kissing new boys. Mom never does, though. Grandma said it's because Mom did all her kissing in college."

I scowled. My mother could be a real pain in the ass. She felt no qualms about saying mean things about me to Forrest. He couldn't understand them as a kid, but eventually he would be able to.

"Pshh. I'm sure your Grandma is right about a bunch of other stuff, but your mom barely kissed anyone at school. I knew her a little bit when she was younger and she was a good girl." Justin sounded like he was smirking but then he suddenly coughed and rushed on. "Not that kissing makes you bad. Damn. It's hard to not say stupid stuff."

"And you swore."

"If we start counting swears, I may as well never speak again, buddy."

I made my presence known and flicked Forrest's light on and off a few times. "Say goodnight to Justin, baby. It's time for a story and bed."

"Can Justin read me my story tonight, Mom?" Forrest came out from under his blanket with his puppy dog eyes in full effect. "Please?"

"Justin doesn't have the book, Forrest."

"I can run over and get it." Justin's eagerness to do such a simple task for Forrest showed me how much he was trying. He sounded so full of hope that I couldn't say no. Not to both of them.

"Come on. I'll toss it down the stairs to you." I grabbed the book from the side table and handed the walkie talkie back to Forrest. "You're going to end up very spoiled, aren't you?"

Forrest snuggled into his bed and wrapped his arm around his stuffed monkey. "Grandpa says I was born spoiled."

I laughed and nodded. "Grandpa is right. I'll be right back."

"I'll be right here!" He watched me leave and then I could hear the sound of his little feet on the floor, hurrying after me. Listening wasn't always his strong suit, clearly. I didn't bother correcting him, fully understanding his excitement to see Justin.

I opened the door and gasped when Justin's chest appeared in my vision. I gripped the book to my stomach and shook my head at him. "You scared the hell out of me!"

His eyes drank in my short pajamas and his lips curved in a hungry smile. "I wanted to see you and waiting at the bottom of the stairs wouldn't give me a good enough view."

Forrest reached around me and grabbed Justin's hand. "Come on! You're already here, Justin! You can just read to me now."

Justin looked like he wanted to come in more than anything but he hesitated. "You'd better ask your mom first. You can't just invite people inside by yourself, Forrest."

Forrest looked up at me. "Can he, Mom?"

I bit my lip and nodded. I had no excuse to refuse him. Forrest wouldn't understand that the reason I didn't think it was a good idea was because it would leave Justin and I alone after he fell asleep. "Sure. Come on in."

Justin slipped past me, his focus shifting to Forrest. "Are there voices I'm supposed to do? I could get away with being subpar over the walkie, but like this? I need to bring my A-game."

I closed and locked the door before following them to

Forrest's room. I tried to see the toy-filled space through Justin's eyes and wondered if he thought I was a slob. I didn't bother with trying to keep the space perfect, not when Forrest was a one-boy-demo team.

I motioned for Justin to sit on the bed next to Forrest and handed him the book. "I do some voices, but Forrest likes to tell me they're not very good. He's a critic."

Forrest giggled. "Mom! All your voices sound like Grandpa's friend. He lost all his teeth and now he sounds funny."

Justin shuddered and pretended to look terrified. "I'm not sure I'm ready for this kind of judgment. Go easy on me, kid. This is my first time reading a bedtime story."

"You'll be better than Grandma. I pretend to fall asleep fast, just so she'll stop reading."

"Forrest!" I laughed, completely shocked by his admission. "You're so sneaky. Maybe when it's time to ground you when you're older, I'll have Grandma read to you all day and night as your punishment. Now I know your weakness."

He shook his head hard and fast while clutching his monkey. "I'll never get in trouble again!"

I looked at the wall clock and grunted. "You'll end up in trouble with Ms. Jenny tomorrow if you don't get to sleep soon. I'll be in the kitchen if either of you need anything."

"I love you, Mommy." Forrest held his hand out to me and I smiled at him. I hoped he never got too old for a hug from his mom.

I tried to ignore how close I was to Justin as I leaned over and hugged Forrest tight. Then I kissed his cheek and nose before doing the same to the monkey. "I love you, too, Forrest. And you, Mr. Red Butt."

Forrest called out when I tried to walk away. "Don't forget Justin!"

I nearly choked. "Oh, Forrest, I don't need to give Justin a goodnight kiss. He's not going to sleep."

"It's fair, Mommy."

Justin grabbed my waist and tugged me between his legs. "It's fair, Violet."

I rolled my eyes but to get it over with quickly, I leaned over and pressed a kiss to his cheek and then I hesitated. Kissing his nose felt more intimate. We were so close already. I could already hear Forrest getting ready to correct me so I lowered my lips and kissed the tip of his nose. I felt his breath against my lips when I pulled back and my entire body heated. "Everything's fair now. Great. You two read and I'll be in the kitchen."

Justin's hands slowly fell away from my body and I could feel his eyes on me as I ran like a coward. I went straight to the fridge and stuck my head in the freezer. I could hear them laughing and then the steady rhythm of Justin's voice as he began reading. When I finally pulled my overheated face out of the freezer, I leaned against the countertop and tried to remember how to breathe normally.

As excited as Forrest was to have Justin reading to him, I knew he could only last so long before passing out. Then Justin and I would be alone and I wasn't sure that was a good idea. I had to protect Forrest from getting hurt, but I had to look out for me, too. Letting myself fall for the guys again was dangerous.

I told myself I wasn't going to allow anything to happen. I was stronger than my desires. I would have

Justin leave as soon as he was done and then I'd go to bed myself. No big deal.

Only, when Justin walked out of Forrest's bedroom and quietly shut the door, I felt the temperature around me climb. He turned and our eyes met and I knew I was a fool for thinking I could ignore the need igniting between us. He slowly walked over to me and when I stood frozen with my body facing the cabinets, he pressed himself into me from behind and braced his hands on either side of my hips.

"Can you be quiet?"

CHAPTER 16
Violet

I swallowed and it sounded like thunder to me. Shaking my head, I licked my lips and spoke through a husky voice. "I… I don't think so."

Justin leaned forward, pressing me over the counter until I was bent completely at the waist with my elbows holding my top half up. He brushed my hair to one side and kissed my shoulder. "I'm going to need you to try."

My thighs quivered as I felt him grind his hard length into my ass. I nearly gasped when he ran his hands down my back and tucked his thumbs into the waistband of my shorts. I gripped the countertop as he tugged my shorts down and left my bottom half bare.

"How many men have touched you since me?" His voice was gravel as he shifted his hips away from mine and slapped my ass. I gasped and he grunted at me while dropping his hand to grab my sex. "Don't wake our son, Violet."

I squirmed under his grip. Justin outside of the

bedroom was charming and kind. He'd been so sweet the night we met, I'd trusted him instantly. Justin inside the bedroom was a different story. He was demanding and firm. He drew out my pleasure like he'd been studying the manual for a few decades. Adding in that he was acknowledging *our* son, I was a goner.

He pushed one thick finger into me and we both groaned together. "I asked you a question. How many men?"

I went up on my toes as his finger stretched me. I didn't want to admit the truth. "That's none of your business."

He reached forward and wrapped his hand over my mouth as he pushed in another finger and began pumping them in and out faster and faster. The slight sting made me want to climb away from him, but there was pleasure in his punishing pace. My body thrummed with it. I panted and lifted one knee higher in an attempt to make more room for his fingers. Justin let out a throaty moan and grabbed the back of my knee to lift it onto the counter. With three of my four limbs on the counter, I was spread out lewdly before him. My thighs burned and my lower lips spread out enough that my clit was completely exposed to the cool air.

He pulled his fingers out suddenly and stroked them over my clit. "All these years and you're still so wet for me. I would have no problem fucking you right now, Vi. You're tight, but you're so wet that your body would open right up for me."

I gasped into his palm over and over again as he thrust his fingers back inside me and used them to fuck me hard and fast. The sound of it filled the kitchen and I squeezed my eyes shut as shame washed over me. Instantly, his fingers stopped and I whimpered.

He dragged my shorts back up and stepped away from me, putting a hefty amount of distance between us. "Fuck. I'm sorry. I just felt you go rigid. I should've asked you if this was okay first. I should've—"

I glanced towards Forrest's door and grabbed Justin's hand so I could pull him to my bedroom. I shut and locked the door behind me and then I walked him backwards until his knees hit my bed and he sank onto it heavily. His face looked haunted until I climbed onto his lap and pulled his arms around me. "I was embarrassed. The sounds... I haven't been with anyone else. That night with you three was the only time for me. I read. I know that things like a lot of wetness are normal... It's just different to experience it."

He slid his hands into my shorts and gripped my ass. "You never slept with anyone else?"

"No. I couldn't."

He stood up and carried me into the bathroom. Turning on the shower, he put me down on the counter and dragged my shirt over my head. My shorts followed and once I was naked in front of him, he stepped back and swore. "I spent the last six years jacking off to my memory of you, Vi. I was sure I remembered every detail of your body after picturing it so many times, but you're even better in real life."

I shifted, uncomfortable with the focus on my body. "Come here."

He dropped to his knees in front of me and pulled my ass to the very edge of the countertop. "You're fucking perfect. I want you to coat my face with your wetness. Let me show you how fucking hot it is."

I gasped when he bit the inside of my thigh and growled into it. He looked up at me with his hair falling into his face and his hazel eyes alight with hunger. It was intoxicating to see him between my thighs, looking at me like he would die if he didn't taste me. He'd filled my own fantasies for years, but having him in real life made all those fantasies seem gray.

Justin pulled my legs over his shoulders and stared at my sex. "That morning we left for work… I took you last. We left you full of my come and begging for more. I had so many plans for you when we got back."

I cried out when he swiped his tongue up the length of my sex. "Justin!"

He tilted his head up and watched me while lazily flicking his tongue over my clit. When I opened my mouth to cry out again, he lifted his mouth and shook his head at me. "You have to be silent, Vi. Do I need to stuff your mouth?"

My mouth watered and I nodded. "Yes, please."

"Fucking hell. You're going to kill me." He balled up my shorts and pushed them past my lips when I opened my mouth. "As much as I'd love to sink my dick into that pouty mouth, I need this more."

I grunted around the ball of silky material and arched my back. I needed more.

He grinned wickedly while running his fingers through my wetness. He lifted those fingers to my nipple and smeared my juices over it before pinching. He covered my clit with his mouth and sucked at the same time and the dueling sensations nearly made me buck Justin off. I screamed into my gag and grabbed a handful of his hair.

He growled against my clit and sank two fingers deep into my core, curling them inside me.

I tugged at his hair while his fingers and mouth filled me with so much pleasure, it hurt. I squeezed my thighs around his head and was so close to coming I couldn't breathe when he abruptly stood up and started ripping his clothes off.

"Need to be inside you. Don't move."

CHAPTER 17
Violet

Justin kicked out of his pants and revealed what I'd told myself couldn't be real. I'd convinced myself over the years I'd built his body up in my head. He couldn't be so physically built and blessed with a beautiful dick, too. Even as one of the first dicks I'd ever seen, I'd known it was perfect.

I balanced precariously on the countertop and then Justin was there, grabbing me and pulling me close. He gripped my ass and held me tight as he thrust his dick in deep. My eyes rolled and I made sounds that would've been shameful if not hidden by the gag. He stretched me and hit so deep I knew, in certain positions, he would hit my cervix with each thrust. I locked my arms and legs around him and dug my nails into his shoulders when he ground himself into me, rubbing against my clit with a perfect friction.

"This. Fuck, Vi. This is where I'm meant to be." He pulled out and slowly thrust deep again. "You were meant for us. Feel this? Nothing else feels like this, Vi."

I gasped when he yanked the shorts from my mouth. "Justin, please!"

He gripped the back of my head and pulled my mouth to his. Teasing his lips over mine, he let me taste myself on his tongue. His thrusts grew faster and I was on the edge of coming again when he pulled out. He kissed me deep once more and then moved me until I was bent over the countertop with my back arched and my face in the mirror. His reverent swear as he looked at me from that angle told me just how sexy he found me.

I met his eyes in the mirror and braced my palm on the glass as he thrust deep again. My mouth fell open and I gasped his name.

He wrapped my hair around his fist and pulled until I straightened and my back was pressed against his chest. Still holding my gaze, he cupped my breasts as he continued thrusting into me. "Look at yourself, Violet. You're so fucking gorgeous. These tits are perfect. Watch them bounce when I take you hard."

I watched his hands slide down to my waist and my breasts bounce with every hard thrust he gave me. I was fighting the need to cry out for him and I was losing that battle quickly.

"You don't get it, Vi. You don't understand the force of nature you are. When I look at you, every part of me burns up and I feel like I'll die if I don't touch you." He stroked down to my sex and he slid his fingers over my clit. "You take me like a fucking goddess, Violet. Look at us."

I forgot how to breathe when he stepped back and lifted my leg over his arm, opening my body up enough that I could see where we were combined in the mirror. I watched his thick length disappear into my core and come out wetter each time. My fluids coated his shaft and watching him stretch me open was somehow both obscene and sexy. When he spread my lower lips apart and let me see what it looked like when he thrust harder, the way my sex spread for him, pushed me over the edge. It was too much.

A scream built deep in my throat as I watched him stroke my clit faster. My body erupted in pleasure and all my muscles clenched down as my orgasm cut off that scream and my breath. I vibrated against Justin as I came hard and I watched in the mirror as he buried himself deep inside me and jerked as his hot come flooded my sex. I watched him empty himself in me and I felt my body milking his cock of every last drop.

Justin managed to get his hand over my mouth just as I sucked in a gasping breath and let out a wild scream of pleasure. He held me tight and kissed my neck and shoulder, his hand still over my clit. It was like he didn't want to let me go and I didn't want him to. I felt like a puddle of good feelings.

He let go of my mouth and cupped my throat instead, caressing his thumb over my racing pulse. "I'll take you to bed. I know I can't stay the night, not until Forrest understands more, but I don't want to leave right away."

I rested my head against his chest and smiled. "Okay."

He picked me up with him still buried deep in me and managed to lay us both in bed the same way. He held me close and spoke against the back of my neck. "The last time I came inside you, Forrest happened."

My pulse jumped and I heard him grunt. His thumb

pressed against my throat with the slightest bit of pressure and I knew he'd felt that jump.

"Does it scare you? The idea of getting pregnant again?" He ran his hand down to my stomach and sighed into my hair. "I wish we could've been there the first time, Vi. I bet you were fucking beautiful with a swollen belly."

I thought about it and realized I had to be as crazy as he was because I wasn't scared. "It doesn't scare me."

"Are you on birth control?"

"No." I took a deep breath and looked back at him over my shoulder. "What is it about you three that makes me absolutely insane? I shouldn't be this careless. It didn't occur to me to worry about it the first time around and I don't care right now, either. Being a single mom is hard and I know that too well now so I should be more careful."

He pulled out, rolled me onto my back, and settled between my thighs with his length buried in me again. Bracing himself on his elbows, he looked down at me with the most serious expression on his face. "You're not a single mom anymore, Violet. The moment you set foot in this town, you were taken. You just didn't know it yet. You can take the time you need to adjust to the idea, but you're ours. You slipped away six years ago, but there's no way in hell we're letting you go again. You and Forrest are home now."

I cupped his face and shook my head. "This is crazy."

"Is it? It feels like the most sensical thing we've done in six years. I was fully in that first night, Violet. *Before* I felt this heaven between your thighs. Afterwards? Forget it. I've been looking for you ever since."

I looked down towards our middles. "You're so sure

that you're ready for a pregnancy?"

He smiled and rotated his hips, making me moan. "I'm fucking sure. Are you?"

Shaking my head, I laughed lightly. "I'm not sure of anything. I wanted this tonight, though. I knew you didn't have a condom on and I was excited about it."

"We'll take care of you. We'll take care of Forrest, you, and whoever else we create." He kissed me and then pressed his forehead into mine. "If we hadn't lost you before, we would've had a huge family by now. You would've spent the last six years knocked-up, being spoiled."

I wrapped my arms around his shoulders. "No matter how crazy you sound, I still want you right here. If we set an alarm and you leave before Forrest wakes up, it'll be like you never spent the night…"

He stroked my cheek and smiled. "If I stay, I'm going to take you again, Vi. Are you sure you can handle that?"

I pushed his hair out of his face. "I've waited six years to feel this good again. I can handle it."

He rolled us over so I was on top. Looking up at me, his eyes widened and he bit his lip. "Fuck. You look good on top of me."

I sat upright, partly shy and partly drunk on promises and pleasure. Cupping my breasts, I rolled my hips and grinned when he swore. "I've only ever been like this with another one of you behind me, pinning me down."

He grunted. "Give it time. Mason and Ben are both dying to touch you again. They're just as crazy about you as I am, Vi. I'm sure they're both pissed at me right now. I had to fight to get the walkie talkie tonight and it was worth it."

"Yeah, you really had fun with that walkie talkie, huh?" Smiling down at him, I rolled my hips again. "I'd hate to send you back to the main house without a good reason for the guys to be pissed at you. I'll have to figure out a way to outshine that walkie talkie."

"What walkie talkie?"

CHAPTER 18
Violet

Jenny called me bright and early the next morning. "I'm sorry to bother you so early, Violet. I was wondering if you'd mind me picking up Forrest for school today. I thought it would give him and my son, Tommy, time to bond."

I'd just gotten out of the shower and had my towel clutched around me while rushing to throw a breakfast together Forrest wouldn't hate. "Oh. Um, sure. I guess that would be fine."

"My Tommy is a little shy. Well. A lot shy. Even though he's been at Lily Elementary since pre-school, Forrest has already made more friends than Tommy has ever been able to. I was hoping Tommy would come out of his shell a bit around Forrest."

I paused with an egg halfway to the skillet. "Wow. Yeah, of course, Jenny. Forrest is such a people person. I'm honestly not sure where he gets it. Lord knows I'm much more of a Tommy."

She laughed. "I'd be lying if I said I was an extravert. Maybe Forrest will rub off a bit on all of us."

I looked over at where he was stumbling around just outside of his bedroom, trying to pull his shoes on. "Thank you, Jenny. I'm sure he'll be excited. You know where I'm staying?"

She laughed. "You're hilarious. This is Lilyfield, Violet. Everyone knows everything about everyone. I was thinking I'd pick him up early and stop by the diner with them. That Chase is a tall drink of water, isn't he?"

"Sure." I wagged my finger at Forrest. "Stay out of the fridge. Ms. Jenny is going to stop by with her son, Tommy. She's going to take you two to the diner."

Jenny heard him cheer and sounded relieved. "I'll be there in ten. Thank you for this."

"Thank *you*. I can go back to sleep for a little while now."

"Jealous." She said something to someone in the background and sighed. "Can I come a little faster? Is Forrest a black hole like my Tommy? I swear I can feed him ten times a day and he'll still get hangry."

"You've seen Forrest. He's a healthy boy. When he gets a little older, I'll need to get a second job to pay for snacks." I checked Forrest out and saw he was fully ready. "You can come whenever. He's dressed and ready to go."

"Thank god. If I have to hear this kid is starving to death one more time, I'm going to scream. I'll be there in a few minutes."

I said goodbye and helped Forrest into his backpack before grabbing a robe. I wrapped it around myself and slipped my feet into my boots to walk downstairs with him.

"Will you pick me up, Mommy?" Forrest looked up at me and yawned. "I want to come home and play with General and Captain. Justin said I could help walk them today."

I brushed his hair out of his eyes and kissed the top of his head. "Of course, baby. I'll be there."

"I love you. Will you read to me tonight?"

My heart warmed and I knelt in front of him. Gripping his hands, I nodded. "Nothing could keep me away. Even if a boat full of pirates tried to stop me, I'd fight them all off to get back to you. I love you, kiddo."

Jenny pulled up in a tiny red car and got out quickly. She rushed around to the passenger side and opened the back door. "Hey, Forrest! Good morning! And good morning to you, too, Violet."

I kissed Forrest once more and stood up. "You all have fun at breakfast. Be good, Forrest. I gave him a twenty, Jenny, so he should be good."

She waved me off. "I invited him. I'm paying. We'll see you this afternoon."

Forrest waved goodbye to me and I stood there for another few minutes, freezing while watching them disappear. Finally, I turned and headed back upstairs. I'd just reached my bedroom when there was a knock on my front door.

My stomach erupted in butterflies. It was probably Justin. I hurried to the door and threw it open, revealing all three men. My mouth fell open and I swallowed. The three of them facing me without anyone around to act as a buffer was intimidating.

"Well? Are you going to invite us in?" Mason winked at me. "It's too early to make me cry, Vi."

I stepped out of the way and motioned for them to come inside. "What did I do to earn this visit? You just missed Forrest. Jenny wanted to give him and her son a chance to become friends so she's taking them to breakfast."

Ben shut the door behind himself and leaned against it. "We saw."

I swallowed nervously and fiddled with the sleeves of my robe. "Well?"

Justin walked to me and stopped with his thighs brushing mine. He'd just left my bed a few hours earlier. I could still feel his erection buried deep inside me, stretching me completely. He slipped his hands inside my robe and cupped my breasts while he leaned down and kissed me.

I groaned as he pinched my nipples and pushed my robe open. With his mouth pressed against mine, I couldn't see what Mason or Ben were doing, but I felt movement behind me.

"What time do you need to be at work, Vi?" Ben gripped my hips and then slid his hands lower to take my robe and slowly work it up my legs.

I stammered as his fingertips stroked over my outer thighs. "Nine…"

Justin dipped his mouth to my breast and pinched my nipple between his tongue and teeth. I gasped and locked my arms around his neck. He sucked hard while stroking my other breast and teasing that nipple with his calloused thumb.

Ben dragged his fingertips over my hips and up my sides while pulling my damp hair to one side of my neck and kissing my bare shoulder. My robe was pinned at my lower back but Ben shifted and it fell to the floor between our feet. He kissed a trail down my spine, his beard as rough as his mouth was soft. He knelt behind me, gripped my hips, and continued those silky stinging kisses over my ass and thighs.

Mason leaned against my couch, watching us. His jaw was tight and his blue eyes were dark as they moved over me. "Two hours is never going to be enough time."

I licked my lips as he pulled his t-shirt over his head and tossed his baseball hat on top of the pile of clothes quickly forming at his feet. "Two hours is a long time."

His smile was wicked as he unbuttoned his pants and slowly walked over to me. "Not with you."

CHAPTER 19
Violet

Justin grunted his agreement as he switched his mouth from one breast to the other. Ben's fingers tightened on my hips as he settled his mouth at the bottom curve of my ass. Tipping his chin forward, he stroked his tongue over the southernmost point of my lower lips. It was a tease, a warming sensation that made me tilt my hips backwards in an attempt to give him more access.

"With you, Violet, we get hard and stay hard. You're human Viagra. Two hours is nothing. Not when there are so many ways to make you scream, so many ways you'll take our cocks." Mason cupped my cheek and ran his thumb over my mouth. Slowly, he pushed it through my lips and rested it on my tongue. "You have no idea how many times I've thought about these lips."

Justin let my nipple pop free of his mouth and stepped away from me. Without him there to hold onto, I slumped forward to my knees. Ben let out a growl of frustration before shifting around behind me and then demanding I raise my hips. I was in a haze of lust but Mason helped me do what he wanted and when he helped me lower myself, it was onto Ben's face.

I yelped and tried to lift myself off of him, but he wrapped his arms around my thighs and pinned me there, with my sex pressing into his mouth. All my fight vanished when his tongue pierced my lips and stroked my slightly swollen inner walls. My mouth fell open and I dropped my head back, releasing a loud moan that might've embarrassed me if my brain hadn't been busy short-circuiting.

Ben growled against my flesh and used his grip on my thighs to spread my legs wider. Fully sitting on his face, I gasped when his nose rubbed my clit. The sensations were overwhelming in the best way.

Still, when Mason stepped forward and cupped my face, I knew what to do, like it'd only been a few days since the last time I'd done it to him. Pressing my forehead against his hard stomach, I used my shaking hands to pull down his zipper and pushed his pants down. I moved them low enough for his shaft to pop free and then I watched as it bounced up and hit me in the chin. My mouth watered as I flicked out my tongue to taste the bead of precum at the tip. Over six years since I'd done that very thing to a man, I knew the act wasn't anything I wanted with anyone else, just the three of them. I'd expected to dislike the motion that first night, especially after listening to my friends talk about it. I'd been wrong. Hearing the men groan and growl for me was one of the hottest things and one of the things I missed the most.

Mason pulled my hair into his fist at the top of my head and stared down at me with a burning gaze as I raised my head and wrapped my hand around his base. Holding his length out, I ran my tongue up and down it, like it was my favorite ice cream cone. His grip tightened when I treated the underside the same way. "Enough, Vi. Open your mouth."

Ben speared his tongue into me faster then and he managed to reach my clit with his fingertips, stroking the nub from the top as his nose bumped it from beneath. I had no choice but to open my mouth as an orgasm rained down on me. Ben showed no signs of slowing down, even as my hips twitched in his arms and I twisted my core over his face as much as his grip allowed.

Mason met my desperate gaze and grunted while slowly feeding me his length. "You know better than to think one orgasm is going to be enough. He's not going to stop until he's drowning in your juices, Vi."

My eyes watered as I struggled to keep my mouth open for Mason while Ben pushed me through one strong orgasm and straight into another. When his tip pressed against the back of my throat, I gagged and clamped my lips down tight on him while I regained my control.

Justin stood next to me and wiped my eyes. "A little rusty, huh? You haven't done this either since us?"

Ben froze beneath me and Mason's length jumped against my tongue. They waited, the air around us growing tighter with their anticipation. I managed to shake my head with Mason still filling my mouth.

"I didn't tell them." Justin held my gaze. "I figured when they found out you hadn't been with anyone since us, they'd want to be close to you."

Ben moved out from under me and pressed his hand to my lower back, forcing me to arch my back and stick my ass out while still stretching tall enough to hold Mason's cock deep in my mouth. "You waited for us."

I heard the rustling of clothes and then felt the blunt head of Ben's cock at my core. It was bigger, hotter, and harder than his tongue, but I knew it was going to feel even better, despite any soreness left over from Justin. I grabbed onto Mason's hips and held Justin's gaze as Ben thrust his full length inside me in one hard stroke. I sucked harder on Mason as the bite of pain from that thrust brought more tears to my eyes. I blinked and they rolled down my cheeks, but the growls of pleasure from them and the feeling of being stuffed full quickly eased the pain into a light sting. It disappeared completely when Ben reached around and cupped my sex, letting his roughened palm grind into my clit.

Ben wrapped his other arm around my chest and held me as he pressed his mouth to my ear. "You don't know what it does to me to know we're the only men that have ever touched you."

Mason gripped my hair tighter and slowly pulled his hips back before sinking to the back of my mouth again. "This mouth? *Ours.*"

Ben growled. "This pussy? *Ours.*"

Justin knelt next to me and smiled. "Your ass will be ours soon, too. Just like that first night."

I grunted around Mason's shaft with each of Ben's hard thrusts. His hips slapping my ass as he fucked me, made almost enough noise to cover the sounds that came from my own throat with each of Mason's deep thrusts. He finally pulled out of my mouth completely and stumbled back. The motion left me unsteady and I fell forward, going flat on my stomach as my slick hands went out from under me.

Ben followed me and shifted his hands to rest on the floor on either side of my face. His hips powered into me harder and faster and with nothing in my mouth, blocking the sound, I released wild sounds of pleasure and cried out his name over and over. He raised up on his arms and drilled his hips into me, fucking me into the floor and scooting me across it, inch by inch.

I scrambled for something to hold onto. My arms flailed out in front of me and I screamed when he rolled his hips. Another orgasm blossomed and I gasped wildly.

Ben widened his legs and the new angle hit even deeper. His thrusts became unsteady and he gripped the back of my neck with one hand. "Come for me, Violet. Come for me while I fuck my come inside you as deep as I can get it."

It was so dirty and possessive, my brain slid down the same pleasure slope as my body. I dug my fingertips against the floor and screamed into my arm. My orgasm was strong enough that it hurt as it tightened everything in me.

When he came, I felt each spray of his come hitting my inner walls. He came forever and with a deep growl. Dropping himself on top of me, he bit down on my shoulder and groaned. "You're ours, Violet. This confirms it."

CHAPTER 20
Justin

Ben rolled off of Violet and Mason pulled her to her feet. He nodded to the bedroom and I followed after them. Ben stumbled in a few seconds later, legs weak from coming so hard. His come was leaking out of Violet as she leaned on Mason and let him put her on the bed. Ben sank into the chair in the corner of the room and watched as Mason knelt on the bed and pulled Violet into his arms. Kissing her hungrily, he gripped her ass and squeezed hard before having her wrap her legs around his waist and lean back on the bed.

Mason groaned in appreciation as he looked down at the way he had Violet spread out. Her head was near the edge of the bed and with one look from Mason, I knew what he had in mind. He gripped her hips and shifted her further up the bed before lining their bodies up and slowly filling her. He held the bottom half of her body and the top half rested on the bed while her head hung over the edge.

I swore in appreciation and moved closer. I watched her eyes widen as she understood the position he'd put her in. She licked her lips nervously and then her face went blank as Mason pulled out and then pushed back in. He braced himself with his hand on her lower stomach and his thumb hooked over her clit. She moaned and when she licked her lips again, it was in hunger.

Carefully filling her mouth with my cock, I swore at the sight of her spread out in front of me. Gripping her breasts, I looked down and watched her pussy stretch around Mason's dick. She was a mess with her own come and Ben's come being forced out of her with every one of Mason's thrusts, but there was nothing sexier.

She gripped my thighs and only gagged once when I brushed the back of her throat. The position she was in gave her no control and left her throat vulnerable. The trust she gave us turned me on even more. I slowly pumped my length in and out of her mouth, listening to the sounds she made as I did. When Mason began fucking her faster, her nails dug into my thighs and those noises doubled.

"Jesus, Vi. Your pussy feels like heaven. I'm not stopping until I flood it with my come." He swore. "Fuck. I felt that, Violet. Your sweet little pussy likes the idea of my come filling it, doesn't it?"

I groaned when she sucked harder on me and moved my hips faster. Bracing myself with my grip on her breasts, I fucked her mouth like I'd dreamt of for so long. Her gargled moans filled the room and urged Mason to fuck her harder. We filled her from either end, stroking into her faster and harder. I watched her puffy and red lower lips drag up and down Mason's dick with each stroke and I watched the pink color of her clit deepen to an angry red as her moans grew into wild screams.

"That's right, Vi. Come on my dick. Come hard." Mason pistoned his hips and flicked his thumb back and forth over her clit until her body arched between us and she flushed a deep red all over.

I pulled out of her mouth and watched as her bruised lips parted wider in a scream that could've woken the dead. Mid-scream, I plunged into her mouth again and growled as my tip slipped into the back of her throat.

Mason didn't slow down. His breathing grew ragged as he continued fucking her through one orgasm and into another. "I'm going to come. Fuck!"

Ben moved to the edge to the bed to watch with his dick in his fist. I pulled out and turned her head so she could see he was there, too. "Look what you do to us."

She cried out our names and then gasped when she felt Mason coming inside her. Her eyes rolled back in her head and I had to watch her come hard again. I couldn't look away from the way her body shook and flushed. The sounds she made were musical while Mason's growls were pure masculine release.

When Mason finished, he stumbled back on his heels and panted. "If you weren't ours before, you sure are now, Vi."

Ben grabbed her legs and pulled her to the side of the bed. He kissed her hard before pushing her to her knees between us. "Finish Justin, Vi. Swallow him."

I moved closer and watched her pull me into her mouth and take me deep. She bobbed her head up and down my length while looking up at me through pleasure-stained eyes. My blood heated even hotter when I saw her dip her fingers between her thighs to rub herself. In no time, I was so close it hurt. "Coming, Vi."

She inched closer and held her mouth on my shaft, showing me she was going to do as Ben said. When my pleasure shot through my body and out of my dick, Violet drank every drop. She sucked me dry and licked me clean like she had back then, too.

As soon as I stumbled out of the way, too sensitive for more attention, Ben stepped into my place and gripped her chin in one hand while still stroking his length with his other. "Make yourself come again, Vi. Rub that pretty little clit faster."

She did as she was told while staring up at him with complete focus.

"Open your mouth." She listened again and Ben hovered with just the tip of his dick resting against her lips. When she tried to take more, he pulled back. "Just this."

She held perfectly still with her lips open just around his tip and her hand flying over her clit. Her breathing changed and her face darkened. When it was obvious she was coming, Ben stroked himself faster and growled out his own release. He flooded her mouth with his come as they came together once more.

"Swallow, Vi." He watched her swallow and then stick her tongue out to show him she'd done what he said. Then, he picked her up and cradled her to his body like she was a child with his arms braced under her ass.

Violet wrapped her limbs around him and held on tight as he gently swayed back and forth. Her eyes were pinched closed, but fat teardrops leaked out anyway.

I wiped her eyes and stroked her hair out of her face. "Are you okay, Vi?"

She blinked those pretty green eyes open and I felt like I'd been punched when she focused them on me. She was stunning and seeing her blink up at me after being thoroughly fucked, tugged at my chest in a way no other woman ever had.

She smiled weakly and nodded. "I'm good."

Mason moved to stand next to her, on her other side. "You're crying."

She let out a breathy laugh. "You'd cry, too, if you just had that many orgasms."

Ben shook his head and moved to sit on the bed. "I might cry because we can't have you for the rest of the day."

Glancing up at the clock, Violet winced and pushed off of Ben's lap. Standing completely bare in front of us, she looked around her room and a smile stretched her lips.

"What?" I couldn't help pressing a kiss to her shoulder. I was halfway hard already and thinking we could get in one more round if we were fast.

"You guys are just like Forrest. There are clothes thrown everywhere." She pulled open her dresser and pulled out a pair of panties and a matching bra. "I need to shower and get dressed for work if I'm going to make it on time. Which, I am."

Ben grumbled. "You don't need to shower."

She tilted her head to the side. "I'm a mess, Ben."

"Good. I want our smell all over you when you're away from us. I want our come slowly leaking out of you all morning so you think about us constantly." He shrugged and bit his lip as he watched her. "I'm not washing you off me, either, Vi. I want to smell you all day long."

She blushed and held her hand to her head. "This is

crazy."

I walked over and slapped her ass. "Crazy would be us hacking into the town's CCTV so we can keep an eye on you when we have to be away from you. Harmony Valley is safe, but still… Our eyes are better than anyone else's."

She shook her head and stepped into her panties. Pulling them over her hips and into place, she grunted. "Happy?"

All three of us scoffed. Mason answered. "Hell no. You're getting dressed. That's the opposite of what makes us happy."

She smiled and slipped into her bra too fast for our liking. "I think I've lost my mind. I'm listening to insanity and I'm going to be bright red at work all day. You're all lucky you're all very beautiful."

I flexed and enjoyed the way her eyes snagged on my arms and my abs. "Beautiful? Really? With these muscles?"

She pulled her work uniform from the closet and pulled it past her chest and down over her hips. When she finished, she was out of breath. Standing in front of us with her body poured into that tiny dress, she was temptation. She took one look at us and swallowed loudly. "Hey. Stop looking at me like that. I have to go to work."

Mason caught her hand and pulled her into his chest. "We've got half an hour to get you there. We can make it work."

She licked her lips and shook her head even as she pressed into him. "It's not long enough. I'll be late."

I moved behind her and tugged her panties to the side. "We'll get you there on time. Scout's honor."

She pressed her hips into me. "Were you a scout?"

I thrust deep into her. "Nope."

CHAPTER 21
Violet

I made it to work at exactly nine o'clock. I was still flushed and sure everyone would be able to take one look at me and see I'd been fucked multiple times that morning. The first few tables I waited on got a very awkward waitress, that much was sure. After no one called me out right away, I slipped into my normal routine and relaxed.

Joanie came in right before lunch, though, and stopped dead in her tracks when she looked at me. Her eyes widened and she slapped her hand over mouth before grabbing me and dragging me into her office.

I stumbled along, checking my face as I went, horrified to think I had something there and no one had mentioned anything. Or something worse. "What is it?"

Joanie closed her office door and whisper-screamed at me. "You had sex with them, didn't you?!"

I gasped and slapped her hands. "What? Shut up! Why would you say that?"

She slapped mine back. "Holy shit. Margaret is going to be insufferable. She's going to think she's the town's matchmaker now. I shouldn't be so happy for you. Not when this is going to make my life harder."

I groaned and tried to straight my messy bun. "We don't have to tell her."

"Oh, she's going to take one look at you and know. You've got a neon sign over your head, telling everyone you just got fucked." She giggled. "And you're walking like you've been riding horses. Has no one else noticed?"

Shaking my head, I flopped into her chair. "No one said anything! Do you think they all knew? Oh, god, Joanie. I have to leave town. This is humiliating."

She snorted. "The hell you're leaving town. You're stuck here with us now. So what if people know you're having sex?"

"With *three* men?!" I pouted. "Joanie, they're going to judge me!"

She flat out laughed in my face. Throwing her head back, she cackled and even pointed at me. "Sorry! Sorry. It's just… No one here is going to judge you for that. Haven't you noticed the number of women to men, Vi? This area has been known for unconventional relationships since it was founded. Haven't you met Gina Davies? She's married to four men. Marly Hill? Married to two men. There are several others. This isn't that kind of place, Vi."

I was shocked silent for a moment. "Really?"

She nodded. "Yes! Women have been juggling men here for decades. If anything, some of the women will be jealous as hell that you got those three."

I cleared my throat and sat up straighter. "I don't know

if I *got* them."

"Judging by the way you're walking? You got them, girl." She grinned even wider. "Those three men are already making it known you're theirs. If the bite marks showing on the back of your neck aren't clue enough, they've growled at every single man who mentions you. Or so I hear."

My heart thudded in my chest. "Did you say bite marks?"

She laughed but tried to turn it into a cough when she saw my expression. "No one shorter than you will be able to see them. That's good news. Right?"

"I'm going to murder them. I asked them if there was anything like that showing before they dropped me off this morning. They swore there wasn't."

"Yeah, well, they lied." She motioned for me to get out of her seat. "In case Chase storms in here, I should actually look like I'm working right now."

"You own the place. What's it matter?" I tried to look at the back of my neck in the small mirror hanging by the door. I couldn't see a thing.

"He's part owner. He was more of a silent partner for the first couple of years, but apparently he's not happy to be silent anymore." She grimaced. "He complains about something I do at least five times a day."

I frowned. "Tell him to kiss your ass. You're amazing. You've been running this place just fine without him and—"

The door behind me opened and bumped me into a stumbling step forward. Chase kept his glare on Joanie while speaking to me. "You've got tables out here waiting to be served."

I winced and looked back at Joanie. She looked like she was ready to burn Chase's body and toss the ashes down the drain. Clearing my throat, I awkwardly inched my way out of the office. "Well, thanks for talking shop with me, Joanie. I'll definitely upsell the customers on…stuff…now."

Chase rolled his eyes and stepped out of my way. "Give your friend better advice next time, Violet. Joanie telling me to kiss her ass isn't going to hurt my feelings."

I paused and looked back at him. Before I could comment on the twinkle in his eye or the increased rage in Joanie's, I heard someone tap the bell for service. Groaning, I turned and hurried to the bar to take a count of who all I needed to check in on.

Immediately, my eyes snapped to the booth in the far corner. Justin, Ben, and Mason were sitting with a beautiful blonde woman who immediately made me feel bad about every extra pound I was still holding onto. My stomach sank. There I was, thinking they were crazy about me, and only me, but I hadn't stopped to think about the fact that maybe they would want more women, the same way I would have more men with them. Maybe one woman wasn't enough for them. I didn't know. I barely knew them at all.

Panic washed over me as I thought about walking away from them. Forrest deserved his dads, so I'd have to see them all the time, even if I moved. I was trapped. They were in my life forever and I was going to lose them to a stunning blonde with zero percent body fat.

"You're staring."

I jumped and clutched my chest. "Coco! How do you do that?"

She leaned against the counter in front of me and glanced over at the guys. "You're staring and you look sad. Why?"

Shaking my head, I forced a smile. "I'm not sad. I was just thinking. What can I get you, Coco?"

"A slice of pie and the truth." She slid onto a stool and watched as I opened the pie case and took out her favorite, cherry. "I'll take some coffee, too. Please."

I added a giant scoop of vanilla ice cream, just like she liked, and poured her a cup of coffee. "I better go check on everyone before they get cranky."

"Coward."

I scoffed at her and made my rounds. I refilled a few glasses and took a few orders before everyone except that far table was taken care of. Knowing I couldn't avoid them anymore, I slowly moved across the diner and crossed my fingers behind my back in hopes I wouldn't cry if they introduced the woman as their other girlfriend.

"That area needs more coverage. It's a blind spot right now." The woman tapped a piece of paper on the table between them. "Also, someone needs to talk to her about following instructions. She's purposefully ignored safety protocols multiple times."

Ben grunted, sounding every bit like an unhappy bear. "She's a fucking child. Why even pay for security if you're not going to take your safety seriously?"

I gently cleared my throat. "I'm so sorry to interrupt. I—"

"You can interrupt all you want." Ben wrapped his arm around my waist and tugged me down on his leg. Smiling up at me, he cupped the back of my head and pulled me closer so he could kiss me.

"Wow." The woman's voice startled me and I pulled away from Ben. "I've never seen you act human before. Color me shocked."

Ben kept his arm locked around my waist and searched my face. "What's wrong?"

"Let me out, Angel." Mason nodded to the blonde woman and I tried not to react to hearing him call her a pet name.

I forced myself to speak to keep things from getting awkward. "I'm fine. Just a busy morning. What can I get you guys to drink?"

Mason slid out after the blonde and pulled me off Ben and into his arms. He ran his hands all over me, but it felt more clinical, like he was searching for injuries. "Did someone do something? Are you feeling sick? Do you need medication for anything?"

Justin and Ben were suddenly surrounding me. Justin pressed the back of his hand to my head. "No fever. I'd feel better if we checked with a thermometer, though."

"Talk to us, Vi." Ben looked like he was close to having his own panic attack.

I cleared my throat and tried to wiggle out of their tight circle. It was useless, though, so finally I just sighed and looked between them at the blonde who was watching us like she'd never seen anything like what she was seeing before. "You're being rude to your lunch date, guys."

The guys and the blonde all reacted at once. First shock and then laughter. Ben jabbed his thumb in her direction. "You thought Angel was our *date*?"

"I'd rather eat my own shit, honey." Angel, apparently her actual name, scoffed. "No sauce."

Mason pressed his lips to the side of my head and

chuckled. "Did you miss our morning? You know? When we claimed you as ours and beat our chests?"

"Violet, you're nuts." Justin pressed a kiss to my mouth before sliding back in the booth. "Certifiable."

I crossed my arms under my chest and waited for them to sit down again. Ben pulled me right back onto his leg. Frowning at them, I grunted. "We barely know each other. I don't know what you three want. For all I know, each of you want your own harem, or something."

Angel rolled her eyes. "These assholes? I'm in serious shock from seeing them be sweet to you. They're normally cavemen who communicate in growls and grunts."

Ben gripped my waist and smiled as he held my gaze. "You're the only thing we want, Vi. You and Forrest."

I swallowed a lump of nerves and emotion. "You barely know me."

"We know enough. What we don't know, we'll learn. We can start with dinner tonight." He saw me start to protest and pressed his finger over my mouth. "With Forrest."

Angel shuddered. "I'm so freaked out right now. This is like seeing your parents make-out."

I pushed Ben's hand away and turned to Angel. "I'm sorry. I'm being rude. I'm Violet. It's nice to meet you."

She grinned. "Angel. I can't wait to tell the guys all about this. No one's ever going to believe Ben can speak normally."

CHAPTER 22
Mason

I looked across the dining room table at Forrest and froze with my fork halfway to my mouth. Setting it back down again, I cleared my throat and glanced at Violet. Had I heard what I thought I heard? "What'd you say, Forrest?"

He looked up at me with his mom's bright green eyes and deep red hair. "I said that General flashed me his butthole so I flashed him back."

Violet's cheeks turned red and she'd quickly turned away from Forrest while she tried to hide her laughter. Her shoulders shook and there was a wheezing sound coming from her as she tried to hold back.

Ben rested his elbows on the table and leaned forward. "Explain a little more, buddy."

Forrest sighed. "He walked by and showed me his butthole. It's the size of a—"

"Okay, Forrest!"

He looked at his mom and shrugged. "I'm just telling

you guys what happened. He lifted his tail and I saw everything. It was disgusting."

I pressed my fist to my mouth. "So... You flashed him back?"

"Yep. But some old lady was walking by and she saw me. She started yelling at me so I came inside. I was just getting General back. She's lucky Captain and I haven't figured out how to turn his farts into bullets yet."

Violet looked horrified. "You flashed an old lady?!"

"No! I flashed General. The old lady shouldn't have been looking." Forrest pouted. "She wasn't supposed to look at my private areas. Be mad at her, Mommy."

I shook my head. "I'm pretty sure you're not supposed to flash your private areas outside."

"General did it!" Forrest pouted. "If I'm in trouble, General should be in trouble, too."

"Forrest." Violet's lowered voice made Forrest sit up and focus on her. "General is a dog, honey. He's always naked. You're a little human. Little humans have to wear clothes. If I find out who you flashed, you're going to have to apologize. I'm sure the last thing she wanted to see was your bare butt on her evening walk. Not that there's anything wrong with it. Your butt is adorable, but it's not meant for strangers on the street. Okay?"

"Mom!" Forrest giggled. "My butt isn't adorable! I'm not a baby. I'm six!"

Ben sighed dramatically. "How could you call his butt adorable, Vi? That's the butt of a six-year-old. Gosh."

She giggled into her hand in the cutest way and then cleared her throat. "So sorry. I don't know what I was thinking. At what age do you think your butt stopped being adorable? I just want to get my records straight."

Forrest looked up and rubbed his chin like he was deep in thought. "Five."

Justin stood up and planted his hands on his hips. "Well, personally, I think my butt is still adorable."

Forrest toppled out of his chair laughing. "No way! You're old!"

I gasped. "If he's old, I'm old and that's just not true."

"You're all old!"

Violet gasped even louder. "Excuse me, young man? You think *I'm* old? How dare you!"

We watched as Violet got out of her chair and gently tackled Forrest to the floor. The thick rug probably protected her elbows and knees but I thought about installing even plusher carpeting to keep them both safe. She easily pinned Forrest and they both laughed while he wiggled out from under her and managed to pin her to the floor. She pretended she couldn't get up and let him count to three, officially winning the match.

Forrest jumped to his feet and did a victory lap around the table, high-fiving us as he went. "I'm the best ever! You're all old and I *don't* have an adorable butt and I'm *not* in trouble for flashing that old lady!"

I easily grabbed him and hung him upside down by his ankles. He laughed and screamed, but I just held him steady and let out an evil cackle. "You may have beat your old mom, but you're going to need a little more practice before you can conquer us, kid."

Violet stood up and frowned. "Now you're calling me old, too?"

Forrest smirked at me from his upside-down position. "Now you're in trouble."

I smiled calmly at Violet. "You're not old. You're a

decade younger than us."

"It's just I could've sworn I heard you call me old." She slowly circled the table, moving towards me.

Forrest crossed his arms over his chest, somehow smug even in his position. "You should run."

I eased him down and he went back to his plate and sat down like he'd never interrupted dinner in the first place. Ben and Justin shrugged and went back to eating, leaving me to deal with Violet. That was fine by me.

"You three stay in here. No one should have to see whatever punishment Vi feels like dishing out." I inched away from the table and squeezed Justin's shoulder. He nodded at me, letting me know he understood what I was getting at. Then, I turned and ran out of the dining room and upstairs, taunting Violet as I went. "You did look a little old in that green face mask the first night."

She chased after me with carefree abandon, the same hidden free spirit she'd been the first night we met. When I ran around the corner in the hallway, I stepped into the laundry room tucked there and grabbed her when she ran past. I barely covered her mouth before a scream escaped and I took a kick to my knee before I got her in the room and shut the door. I pinned her to it with my hips and jerked her arms over her head, pinning her wrists to the door as well.

She panted and tugged at her hands. Her hips jerked against mine and we both groaned together. "Mason..."

I held both her wrists with one hand and lowered my other hand to cover her mouth. Brushing my mouth against her cheek, I whispered. "Can you stay quiet?"

Her eyes were feral as they searched mine. She shook her head.

"Do you want to try?"

Those pretty eyes fluttered and her breath caught. I didn't make her nod. I knew what she wanted. Running my hand down her throat and chest, I cupped her breast and licked my lips.

"You should only be allowed to wear skirts around us. Anything else is too much." I pushed her leggings and panties down her thighs and cupped her sex to find her slick with desire. Dropping to my knees, I growled just before burying my face into her wetness. Her folds were silky and hot, her taste like my favorite honey. I could've drunk from her all day and night long.

Her head thumped against the door and she whimpered. "*Mason.*"

Shoving her clothes the rest of the way down her legs, I tilted my head to eat her the way I wanted to. Sucking her lips, I groaned into her sex as more of her sweetness flooded my mouth. Swiping my tongue from front to back, I spread her out and curled my tongue into her tight little hole.

"*Mason!*" Violet yanked at my hair, her voice desperate.

Knowing I didn't have all the time I wanted, I twirled my tongue in her a few times and then closed my mouth over her clit. Flicking her little bud, I ran my fingers through her wetness and circled my pointer finger over her ass, adding pressure as I tongued her faster. Glancing up at her, I saw her mouth fall open and her eyes go wide.

I snapped my other hand up to cover her mouth just as she started to cry out. Pressing my fingertip past the tight ring of her ass, I closed my mouth over her clit and sucked hard. She came instantly, shaking and grinding her sex into my mouth harder until it was too much for her. When she jerked her hips away, I swore with the desperate need to push her to another orgasm. I wanted to eat her pussy until she begged me to stop.

Leaning back, I ran my fingers over her soaked lips and watched her face. "Fucking perfect."

She blushed and dropped to her knees. "Let me take care of you."

I looked down at my painful erection and shook my head. "We've been gone long enough. Go on down."

She pouted and shook her head. "I can be fast."

Squeezing my eyes shut to block out the sight of her begging, I shook my head again. "Get back to Forrest, Vi. You can take care of me later."

Her pout deepened but she stood up and pulled her clothes on. "I want to take care of you now."

"You're pouting a lot for a woman who just came all over my face." Standing, I adjusted my hard-on in my pants and then gripped the back of her head. Pulling her mouth to mine, I kissed her hard, letting her taste herself. She melted into my chest, going pliant for me just the way I loved. I wrapped my other arm around her and held her soft body against my own. "I don't want to let you go."

She pressed kisses to my chin and down the front of my throat. "I don't want you to."

Growling, I eased her away from me and nodded at the door. "Go, Vi. I'll be down in a few minutes."

She slowly backed away and glanced down at my pants. "Are you going to—"

"*Woman*. You're killing me. I'm trying to be responsible." I took a ragged breath and backed away from her. My hands shook with the need to grab her and yank her back to me. "I don't want our son to think I'm a creep before he gets to know me."

Her eyes softened as she gazed up at me with a crooked smile on her face. "He's already crazy about you, Mason. Like mother, like son."

I stared at the door after she slipped out and walked over to press my forehead against it while grinding my teeth together. I wanted to chase her down and rut her wherever we landed. I wanted her pregnant with more babies and I wanted her under our roof with our son. Maybe we didn't know everything about each other, but I knew that she was meant to be ours.

CHAPTER 23
Violet

After dessert, we all decided to walk General and Captain together. Captain had managed to steal a whole slice of cake while no one was watching and he'd shared just enough with General that the farts were filling the house with toxic fumes. I felt bad for the guys. They had to go back inside and live in an enclosed space with General.

Mason and Justin were jogging with Forrest and General, all four of them burning off cake energy. Ben and I walked Captain at a slower pace. I didn't know if Ben felt as sick as I did after gorging on the delicious cake, but I had a feeling Captain was right there with me. Neither of us were going to ever lose those last few pounds if we kept eating cake like we were. It did make me feel extra attached to the dog, though. Being around the guys, I was surrounded by muscles and tight asses. I needed Captain to feel like I even remotely fit in.

Ben had finally let me have Captain's leash, but he kept

his hand on my lower back with a fistful of my sweater bunched in it. It seemed he was terrified Captain was going to drag me away. Captain was being great, though.

I smiled down at the giant dog and patted his head. "You're such a good boy, Cap. Don't let Ben make you feel like you're not. You hear me? You're a good boy."

Ben held my sweater tighter and grunted down at me. Walking down the sidewalk next to me, he somehow felt even larger as he kept me away from the street, using his mass as though he could protect me from a car if it came our way. "He dragged Justin once. He saw a squirrel and took off before Justin noticed, so Just wasn't ready. I happened to look out the window and saw Justin flying by. Literally."

I giggled. "Was he okay?"

He pulled me to a stop as we came to a tiny road we needed to cross. "Nice try, trying to pretend like you were worried about him. I'm going to tell him you laughed before checking on him."

I leaned into his side and smiled. I'd been doing that so much my face was starting to hurt. "Obviously, I can see that he's fine."

Ben stroked his hand into my hair and leaned down until we were eye to eye. "You're so beautiful, Vi."

My heart thumped wildly in my chest. "Where'd that come from?"

He searched my face and slowly kissed me, moving his mouth over mine gently, like I was something precious to be cherished. When I let out a breathy sigh, his knuckles dug into my back and I felt his body stiffen while he held me even tighter. Tipping his head back slightly, he met my eyes. "I've looked twice at every red head I've seen since meeting you, hoping one of them would be you. You have no idea what that was like. So, when I see a red head in front of me now and it's actually you, I feel like fucking cheering, Vi. Instead of feeling disappointed like I have every time for the last six years, I feel elated. I can't look at you and not think about how beautiful you are."

I stared up at him with my mouth agape. I was speechless. No one had ever said anything like that to me and I was smitten. More than.

He cleared his throat and loosened his hold on me. "So, yeah. That's where it came from."

I stretched up on my tip toes and kissed him. Gripping the front of his shirt, I rubbed my nose against his in a gesture that was probably *way* too much. "I do know what that was like. I looked for you, too. Each time a man approached me who wasn't one of you three, I felt like screaming. Everyone else was a disappointment."

He slid his hand down to my ass. "I fucking hate that men approached you. I hate we weren't there to rip their arms off for even thinking of touching you."

Smiling, I raised my eyebrows. "If I allowed myself to think of the women you *did* touch, I'd probably feel like ripping things off, too. I don't want to borrow trouble, though."

His face fell. "If I'd known there was a chance of finding you… Things would've been different."

"Ben, it's okay. You didn't owe me anything. I'm not upset about any of that stuff. If I'd ever found anyone attractive and slept with them, I know you all would be the same."

His grip on my ass tightened. "I wouldn't be so sure about that. You don't understand how much it satisfies every caveman urge in us to know that no other man has ever seen you naked or touched you. To know that all of you is one hundred percent ours... It's a heady feeling, Vi."

A loud growl from beside us drew our attention and I jumped. Looking down at Captain, I found him staring up at us, stomping his feet. I laughed and stepped away from Ben. "We'd better keep walking before he really throws a tantrum."

Ben resumed his grip on my sweater and grunted. "He's ruining my vibe right now."

I rested my head on his arm as we resumed walking. "Your vibe? Have you tried shooting him a DM about it?"

Up ahead, I saw Forrest running down the sidewalk, back towards us. His smile was stretched so wide across his face I felt like I could see every single one of his teeth. General was running behind him with Justin and Mason. My heart felt so full watching him run with the men he'd deserved as fathers his whole life.

Suddenly, I was jerked forward. I screamed but it was cut off mid-way through when I was yanked back into Ben's chest. My arm felt like it was being ripped off as Captain continued forward. Ben growled as he grabbed the leash and pulled Captain to a stop but the damage was done. My arm throbbed painfully and tears filled my eyes.

"Captain, stop!" Ben eased the leash from around my wrist and ran his hand over my face. "How bad is it?"

My motherly instincts kicked in when I heard Forrest cry out. I snapped my head around to him and saw him on the ground, holding his knee. Pushing away from Ben, I ran towards Forrest, forgetting my own arm completely. When I got to him, he was full out crying with giant tears rolling down his cheeks.

I dropped to his side and gently pried his fingers away from his knee. "Let me see it, baby."

He whimpered and more tears flowed freely. "I tripped!"

I frowned when I saw the rip in his pants and blood already staining the khakis. I pressed a kiss to his head and cupped his cheeks. "Another wound for the books, huh? You're going to get to create a really great story to explain this scar when you're older. Let's get you home and cleaned up. Okay?"

He held his arms up to me and I grabbed him up without a second thought. The pain in my arm made me clench my teeth and suck in a sharp breath through my nose. Ignoring it, I held him against my hip and started back towards the house.

Ben stepped in front of me. "Let me carry him. Your arm, Vi."

I shook my head. "I've got him. It's okay."

"*Violet.*" He reached for Forrest and clenched his jaw when Forrest held onto my neck tighter. "Forrest, let me carry you, buddy. Captain hurt your Mom's arm."

Forrest hesitated and then reached for Ben. I watched with a different kind of pain in my chest. I needed Forrest to still need me. Seeing him let Ben take care of him made me anxious.

My feet went out from under me and I gasped until I realized Justin was picking me up. Carrying me bridal style, he looked down at me and ran his eyes over my arms. "We saw General yank you. You okay?"

"I'm fine. I can walk, Justin."

Mason walked next to us with General by his side.

"Just let us take care of you."

Looking back at where Ben was walking away with Forrest, I swallowed. I wasn't sure I could do that.

CHAPTER 24
Mason

Inside the house, Ben carried Forrest to the kitchen and put him down on the island. I grabbed a pair of scissors from the junk drawer and paused with them next to the boy's leg. He stared at the scissors with wide eyes and his bottom lip wobbled.

I ruffled his hair gently. "We're going to turn these pants into shorts so we can see your knee better. Don't worry, though. We'll buy you some new pants."

Justin put Violet on the counter next to Forrest and she immediately tried to climb down. He pressed his hands to her knees and shook his head. "Stay."

Her eyes narrowed on him. "I'm not a dog."

"Our dogs listen better." Shaking his head, Justin growled under his breath. "I'm going to grab an ice pack. If you're not sitting right here when I get back, we're going to have a problem."

We all watched to see what was going to happen, even Forrest. When Justin turned his back, she stuck her tongue out at him but she stayed where she was. Ben grunted from beside me. I just shook my head with a smile.

I cut Forrest's pants into shorts and checked out the damage to his knee. He had a good few inches of road rash and there was a slightly larger cut that was responsible for most of the bleeding. I clucked my tongue and looked into Forrest's wide green eyes. "I think we'll be able to save it, soldier. It's going to be a good day, after all."

He almost laughed but fear kept him tight-lipped. He looked over at his mom and then back at me. "Mommy always kisses it better."

My heart stopped in my chest for a beat. Seeing the tiny little human in front of me that I'd helped create, and hearing him talk about his booboos being kissed better, nearly crushed me. We'd missed so much. How many skinned knees had we missed? How many times had we missed the chance to kiss his injuries better?

I never wanted to miss another chance with my son again. Leaning down, I gently kissed the side of his knee that wasn't scraped. I felt awkward doing it at first, knowing everyone was watching me, but I figured I hadn't done it too wrong when no one screamed at me. My eyes came up while I was still bent over and met Violet's. Hers were suspiciously moist.

Clearing my throat, I straightened and smiled at Forrest. "It's not a Mommy kiss, but I hope it helped a little bit."

He nodded slowly and a small smile stretched his lips. "Mommy also gives me five dollars and a bucket of candy."

Ben and I were both already reaching for our wallets when Violet scoffed. "No, sir, I do not. Don't tell fibs,

Forrest."

He sighed. "Sorry."

Justin came back in and handed me the first-aid kit. He put his own black bag down next to Violet and wedged himself between her knees. He lifted the bottom of her sweater up and over her head, leaving her in just a bra on our kitchen island. He paused with his hands mid-air. "Where's your undershirt?"

Violet slapped his stomach and grabbed her sweater to cover herself. "Why would you assume I'm wearing an undershirt?"

He cupped the elbow on the arm that had been tugged around and held it still. "I just assumed... This sweater is thin. Don't you need layers for warmth?"

She looked over at Forrest and saw we were all watching. Her cheeks darkened. "How's your knee, baby?"

I jerked myself out of my stupor and cleared my throat so I could speak again. There wasn't anything I could do about the reaction threatening to form in my pants. Dragging my eyes away from her bare shoulders and chest, I opened the kit and started pulling things out.

"It hurts." Forrest was quiet for a moment. "Are you okay, Mommy? Did Captain hurt you?"

Violet gasped dramatically. "Captain? Never! He wouldn't hurt a fly. I'm fine. I just wasn't paying attention and Captain was so excited to see you and General."

"You were kissing Ben."

Violet stammered for a few seconds and then calmly nodded. "You're right. I was. How do you feel about that?"

I held my breath as I waited for his answer. I could tell Ben and Justin were doing the same.

Forrest shrugged. "I don't care."

Ben let out a breath that sounded more than a little relieved. "Okay. Good."

I looked down at Forrest's knee and then looked over at the spray I'd need to use to clean the wound. I'd taken care of wounds in the field while bullets sprayed the ground around me without a single shake to my hands. Something about knowing I was going to have to cause pain to my son gutted me, though. My hands shook and my stomach clenched.

Violet reached over and put her hand over mine. "I can do it."

Shaking my head, I squared my shoulders and met Forrest's eyes. "I've got this. Forrest is going to help me. Right?"

He nodded. "I can help."

While Justin checked Violet's arm, I worked on cleaning and bandaging Forrest. He was tougher than I was when I put the cleaner on his tiny knee. I wanted to crawl into a hole and never come out when I saw the tears in his eyes. By the time I was finished, I'd used a ridiculous number of bandages and his knee was triple the size it should've been.

Justin had checked Violet to make sure she was okay and they both stared at me staring at Forrest's knee, smiles on their faces. My shoulders were stiff and I felt like I'd just detonated a bomb. They seemed to find it hilarious, though.

Ben slapped my shoulder. "Ignore them. I feel a little sick, too. We've all taken care of gunshot wounds and worse, but watching you do that was awful."

Justin grunted. "Well, my diagnosis is that you'll be sore

as hell for a few days. No more walking General for you. And you, Forrest, were a great patient. If I were you, I would've screamed just to scare Mason."

Forrest held out his arms for me and when I hugged him, he squeezed me tight. "I can't scare Mason. He was a good doctor."

I tried to keep my emotions in check while holding him. I doubted he would understand the excitement I felt at hearing his words. I hoped he would one day.

CHAPTER 25
Violet

Sitting across from Margaret and next to Joanie and Lizzie, I wondered if there were other towns like ours, where women were holding secret meetings to plan events to take down the town mayor. I highly doubted it. Joanie gripped my knee every so often, just when Margaret or Brenda said something extra wild, but Lizzie seemed unphased by her aunt's besties.

"This event is going to be huge. Mayor Stevens talked it up with some of his golf club buddies and they're all horny for it." Margaret rolled her eyes and Joanie gripped my knee tighter. "We're going to make it a town-wide event. Maybe it'll even be an annual event if the guys can't get it through their thick skulls the first time around."

Eve looked tired as she spoke up. "What are we going to be doing? Some kind of race? I've got to tell you right now, if it's a race, I'm not your girl."

I nodded along. "Yeah, I should back out now if it's a race. I'd just bring the team down."

Margaret shook her head. "No, this isn't going to be some boring battle. We're all going to come up with challenges. Mayor Stevens said he was going to talk to the guys about coming up with some, so we need to come up with some good ones, too."

"Wearing a period simulator for fifteen minutes!" Gertie Holland, the stylist, jabbed her finger in the air. "No! Thirty minutes!"

"They should be forced to walk around in heels to make their ass look sexy!" Joanie groaned. "My toes are punched half to death right now."

"Cook a whole meal while holding a baby!"

"Clean the house after working a double!"

"Paint their fingernails without messing up."

"Do yoga!"

"Apply perfect makeup and not sweat it off!"

"Do their hair every single day!"

The list went on and one with the women throwing all out the idea of things that we had to do but didn't think the men would be able to. It was early in the morning or I was sure the ideas would've been less stereotypical. We were all running off of our first sips of caffeine and coming from just having to get ready for the day.

After a night of wondering if I could sneak the guys into my room, I'd woken up without my full brain function that morning. I hadn't been able to, so I'd spent the night tossing and turning. Somehow, I was already spoiled. I wanted to cuddle.

Sighing a little too loudly, I drew unwanted attention my way. Looking around quickly, I swallowed and smiled. "I'm really good at crafting. Maybe we should have some kind of crafting battle."

Margaret stared at me long after the others looked away and started talking amongst themselves about different ideas. Everyone seemed excited about the idea of battling the men for some reason. Margaret's eyes slowly narrowed and she nodded to herself. "It's my night to hang out with Forrest, isn't it?"

My cheeks heated when everyone looked at me. "Um. You don't have to do that."

Joanie patted my thigh. "Let her! I need a night away from the diner. We could go to the bar and relax a little. I would die for a night to get away from Chase. He's at the diner all the time and now he's hanging out on his porch every night, which happens to look right into my windows. I can't help but see him."

I didn't get a chance to say anything before Margaret rushed on. "That sounds like a brilliant plan! Maybe a few of you women should go out together. You deserve it. I can stick around to watch whoever needs watching."

Billie looked over at us hopefully. "A night away from my cabin surrounded by my bosses sounds really great."

I wanted to stay home and spend time with the guys but I didn't want to let the women down. "Okay, sure. As long as you don't mind watching Forrest, Margaret."

She waved me off and stood up. "Okay, everyone. Keep coming up with ideas for the battle. We'll have another meeting when I know a little more."

Billie walked over to me as soon as everyone started standing to leave. She smiled brightly, but it didn't quite reach her eyes. "I hope it was okay I invited myself. If not, I can just—"

"Don't be ridiculous. Of course, it was okay. I might be a hostage to the night, so come at your own risk, I guess."

I smiled back at her. "If you get tired of hearing me complain about being tired, just leave me to my own devices."

Joanie put her arm over my shoulders. "We would never leave a friend behind."

"A friend leaving me behind at Jack's is how Forrest came to be." After I said the words, I realized how much of an overshare that was. "Sorry. I don't know what's wrong with me lately. I think the filter between my mouth and brain is on the fritz."

"That seems like a good story to hear tonight over a few shots of whiskey." Billie glanced down at her watch and groaned. "I have to go. Work calls. Should I just meet you guys there?"

We settled the details and Joanie and I walked to the diner together to start our day. She went to the back and I stopped behind the counter to pull on my apron and grab my order pad. I took over for the waiter who opened the diner and served the early morning customers. His name was Brian and he rarely said a word to anyone, but he didn't need to in order to be good at his job.

I worked through the morning and then spotted the guys coming in around lunchtime with a man I didn't recognize. They went to the same booth they always went to and I walked over to see what they wanted. And to see them. It scared me to admit that I'd missed them the night before.

Justin looked up and grinned at me when I got closer. Pulling me onto his lap, he tipped me back and kissed me within an inch of my life. When he let me up, I was breathing heavily and my heart was racing. My panties were definitely uncomfortably damp, as well.

"Hi, Vi. You're a sight for sore eyes." He nuzzled his nose into my hair and kissed my neck. "Missed you."

I sank into him even more. "I—"

"Sorry, guys!" Joanie came strutting towards their booth. "Look your fill now because you don't get Violet tonight. We're going to the bar."

I shot her a look and tried to keep my face from turning red. "Margaret volunteered to watch Forrest. So, I guess I am going out for the first time since I moved here."

The guy with Justin, Mason, and Ben threw his head back and laughed, stopping Joanie from whatever she was going to say. "Angel was right. This is wild. I've never seen my bosses pout before, but *wow*. It's a sight."

Mason grumbled under his breath at the other guy before turning back to me. "This is Morgan Heath. He works with us at our agency. He thinks he's hilarious."

I nodded at Morgan. "Nice to meet you, Morgan. I'm Violet."

Ben ignored everything else but me. "Forrest won't be at home and you're going out to a bar? Are you sure?"

Joanie nudged me with her hip. "They *are* pouting."

Justin sighed into my neck. "Just a little."

CHAPTER 26
Violet

Jack's was a hole in the wall bar with sticky floors, the perpetual smell of Axe body spray, and not enough lights. It was amazing, though. It was the only bar in Harmony Valley so it was always packed and full of friends. I'd sent Forrest to play video games with Margaret and made her promise she wouldn't let him play, or play herself, any terrifying games that would give him nightmares. I doubted she listened to me. I hadn't been able to say goodbye to the guys before Joanie was parked in the driveway, honking at me.

We sat eerily close to the table I'd sat at all that time ago and Billie joined us soon after we arrived. We all ordered a shot of whiskey and a beer before we started talking. It only took a few minutes for Billie to feel like a forever friend. She fit in with Joanie and I perfectly and we were laughing about something silly that happened with the ease of three women who'd known each other for a lifetime. It was fun and I didn't regret going out with them.

Even if I did miss the guys a little.

Joanie leaned forward and grabbed my arm. "There's a guy coming over here for you."

I snorted. "While I'm sitting next to the two of you? Yeah, right."

She rolled her eyes at me. "He's honed in on you. Just wait. He'll be here in three...two..."

"Hey, beautiful." I turned and found a handsome enough guy standing much too close to me. He ran his eyes down my body and smiled. "Wow... I'm sorry. I don't mean to stare, but you're something else."

I snorted; I couldn't help it. I didn't know what to say, either. I'd been hit on while in college, but there'd been so many years of single mom-hood I just felt awkward with the guy looking at me like I was a beautiful cut of steak.

"Would you like to dance?" He inched even closer and his eyes went down the front of my dress.

I leaned away from him and shook my head. "No, I'm sorry. Thank you, though. I'm just not a dancer."

He put his hand on the table and kept right on smiling at me. "We don't have to dance. We can just talk. I'm Jimmy."

I glanced over at Joanie and Billie for help, but they'd been distracted by a couple of guys themselves. Feeling like running away, I had to force myself to sit still. "I'm seeing someone else. No hard feelings."

He put his other hand on the chair, right next to my back. When he brushed along my skin, his smile grew even wider. "Come on, pretty lady. Just let me show you a fun time tonight."

I dropped my smile. "No. Thank you. I just want to hang out with my friends."

"I can be your friend." He finally made his move, leaning forward and brushing my hair behind my ear.

As I was swatting at his hands to get them away from my face, I heard growling and then Jimmy and his slimeball hand were gone. I blinked and looked around, feeling like I was losing my mind. Then I spotted Ben's wide back. He was marching Jimmy out of the bar.

I gasped, not wanting Ben to get in trouble, and looked at Billie and Joanie. They were talking to their guys, but I blurted out what I had to. "Ben's here. I think he's going to kill that guy who was hitting on me. I'll be right back!"

I hopped off my stool and rushed after them. Ben was easy to find. He looked like a professional footballer walking through the crowd. It wasn't easy for me to part the sea of happy people the way it was for Ben. I struggled. By the time I got to him, he was tossing Jimmy out the front door of *Jack's* and walking out after him.

I grabbed Ben's arm and tugged. "Where are you going?"

He looked back at me and then at Jimmy, before sighing and walking me back inside the bar with his hands on my hips. His eyes were laser focused on me. "He was touching you."

I nodded. "He was. I had it handled, though."

He'd backed me right onto the dance floor. "Dance with me."

My stomach fluttered. "You wanna dance with me?"

He nodded and pulled me into his chest. "You're ours, Violet."

I rested my hands on his shoulders and bit back a sound of pleasure when both of his hands rested just over my ass. "You keep saying that."

He pulled me even closer and let me feel how hard he was. "Because it's true. Tell me you don't feel it."

"Of course, I feel that. A dead woman could feel that." I glanced around to see if anyone was looking at us but everyone seemed lost in their own worlds. Looking back up at Ben, I let myself experience how I truly felt at seeing him. My smile stretched wide. "What are you doing here?"

"I just wanted to make sure you were okay." He frowned towards the door. "Not all the men here are gentlemen."

"You were worried about me?"

He nodded. "You're special. Any man with half a brain would see you and want to take his chance."

I laughed easily. "And what? You're here to stop them?"

His expression was serious. "Yes."

"Ben!" I moved my hand down to rest over his heart. "That's crazy. You can't follow me around and keep men from hitting on me. Not that I think I'm going to have all that many men lined up. It's just crazy. You have a life!"

He shifted his hands lower and cupped my ass. "Until everyone in this town knows you're ours, we'll do what we have to, to make sure no one else gets too close. We already lost you once. We know exactly what that feels like and we don't want that again."

I took a deep breath and blew it out slowly. "You know I felt it, too. I don't want that again, either. You don't have to go around throwing men out of bars."

"I do." He cupped my ass tighter and let me feel the hard length of his cock pressing into me through the layers of our clothing. "No one else gets to touch you."

I bit my lip and tried to look calmer than I felt. "What

if I don't like this macho man stuff? Or how possessive you are?"

He leaned down and pressed his mouth to my ear. "I can feel the heat of your pussy trying to burn me up through your clothes, Vi. You can lie to me, but *it* can't."

I nearly choked on my shock, but he was right. His words caused a flood of moisture to gather between my thighs. "Okay, fine. You know I don't hate your macho attitude."

"The real question is, just how much do you like it?" He stepped away from me and gave me a look that could've started a grill, it was so hot. Then, he walked away.

I stood there for a few seconds, watching him head towards the bathrooms in the back. I felt I was going crazy for a moment. Was he really hinting at me following him? Glancing back at the table I'd been at with Joanie and Billie, I saw they were deep in a conversation with another couple of men. They weren't missing me.

With my heart hammering away, I took a deep breath and hurried after Ben.

CHAPTER 27
Ben

Jack's back hallway held two bathrooms, a door that led to the kitchen, and a door that led to his office. Unfortunately for Jack, he didn't lock his office door and I knew for a fact he was out of town for the night. I waited in the shadows, unsure if Violet would follow me, but ready for her if she did. I hoped she did. Seeing men glance at her in her pretty dress had been killing me. I was going to leave her alone and go back home until Jimmy touched her. After that, I couldn't help it. I needed to erase his touch from her skin.

A slow smile stretched across my lips as I spotted Violet. She glanced over her shoulder and then hurried into the dark hallway. I reached out and grabbed her arm, pulling her into Jack's office with me. Clamping my hand over her mouth, I kicked the door shut and locked it before pinning her to it. Face to face, I stared into her wide eyes and watched as she recognized me and melted.

I kept my hand over her mouth as I ran my other hand

down her waist and hip until I could slip under her dress and trail my fingers up the inside of her thighs. The heat from her sex greeted me like an old friend and when I slipped my hand inside her panties, she let her head fall back against the door.

Her wet pussy welcomed my fingers with a tight squeeze and more of her juices flowing down my palm. I scissored my fingers inside her core and held her body still with mine. Pressing my mouth against the skin just under her neck, I nipped and sucked while whispering to her about what I was going to do to her. "After I stretch you out, I'm going to bend you over that desk behind me and fuck you like the animal you make me feel like, Vi. I'm going to fuck you until I forget the sight of another man touching you."

She mumbled into my hand but it was incomprehensible. She wasn't waiting for me to figure it out, though. She pushed my hand away and dropped to her knees between me and the door. Gripping my pants, she looked up at me with her pretty eyes wide and innocent. "I just want to do this first."

I swore up at the ceiling before looking back at her. "Do whatever you want, Vi. I'm yours."

She tugged my belt off and then unbuttoned and unzipped my pants while looking directly into my eyes. Pushing them down to my knees, she did the same with my briefs before taking my painfully hard erection in her hand and stroking it. Holding it tightly, she stroked it a few more times before opening her mouth and flicking her tongue out to stroke the tip.

I groaned and braced my hands against the door. "Fuck, Violet."

Without any more preamble, she opened her mouth and took my length in deep. All the way to the back of her throat, she sucked me in and held me there while holding my gaze. It felt like heaven. Like a warm, wet heaven made of silk. Then she ran her tongue back and forth along the underside and I saw stars.

Violet ran her hands along my thighs and up to my ass before cupping my balls. She pulled her mouth back so she could suck just my tip and she flicked her tongue over the slit until I gripped a handful of her hair and pulled her back to her feet. Her eyes were wild as she frowned at me. "I wasn't done."

I spun us around and backed her up to Jack's desk. Her ass bumped into it and something fell over, but I didn't give a shit. "*I* was almost done. Your mouth is too good and I need to fuck you. Understand?"

Tipping her head back, she offered me her mouth and let out a growl of frustration when I bypassed her mouth and kissed her shoulder instead. That growl turned to a moan when I sucked and bit her shoulder and neck. She wrapped her leg around my hip when I got to her throat and left my mark all over her pretty flesh.

I wrapped her hair around my fist and tugged her head back. Leaning down, I brushed my mouth over hers but when she tried to take more, I pulled back. Over and over again, I teased her. Her fingers dug into my arms and when she could do nothing else, she arched her back and rubbed her core against my dick in a move that made my breath stutter. I crashed my mouth against hers and kissed her until we were both breathless.

I reached down and grabbed her waist to put her on the desk. More things fell over but neither of us paid it any attention. I shoved her dress up around her waist and pulled her panties to the side while we kissed desperately. She braced herself on the desk behind her and screamed into my mouth when I thrust my entire length into her.

Violet wrapped her legs around my waist and moaned when I straightened to look at her, spread out for me. Buried in her as deep as I could get, I grabbed the top of her dress and tugged it over her shoulders and down her arms. Dragging it over her breasts, I bent down and buried my face between them, inhaling the fresh scent of her skin while rubbing my mouth across every inch I could reach.

"You didn't wear a bra." I rolled my hips and looked up at her face to see it pinch in pleasure.

She licked her lips and shook her head. "Can't with this dress."

I sucked one of her nipples into my mouth and clamped it between my teeth. She gasped and I bit down harder until that gasp turned into a breathy moan. "If any other man watched the way your tits sway when you walk, I'll hunt them down, Vi. These are mine."

Her arms gave out and she went flat on the desk. Immediately, her hands were in my hair, holding my head to her chest. "Fuck me, Ben. *Please.*"

I pulled out completely and reached down to rip her panties off so I could stare at her naked sex. She was swollen, wet, and pink, so ready and needy for me. Ignoring her protests, I knelt in front of her and spit on her pussy before pushing my spit deep inside her with two fingers. "You don't know half of the dirty shit I want to do to you, Vi. I want to own you."

She watched me with wide eyes as I stood back up and notched my dick head at her opening. Her lip was caught between her teeth and she was cupping her breasts, pinching her nipples.

"It's only fair when you own me so completely." With that, I slid home and grabbed her hips. "Brace your feet on my chest, Violet. I'm going to fuck you now."

She did as I said and screamed my name with my first withdrawal and thrust home. Her body shook with the force and the desk scraped the floor as it shifted. Her eyes were wild as they held mine. "Yes!"

Wrapping my arms around her thighs, I held on tight and lifted her ass slightly as I fucked her. Hard and fast, I took her like I needed to. The desperate feeling I'd felt when Jimmy touched her, the hunger I'd felt when I saw her leave the garage in her pretty dress, I let her have it all. My balls slapped against her ass and my cock hit a spot that she loved. It had her coming almost instantly.

Violet's pussy clamped down on my dick and she shook under me. Her screams were loud and she jerked back and forth, knocking things over as she did.

I fucked her through her orgasm and another, demanding more from her body. When I felt myself getting closer, I wrapped her legs around my waist and leaned over her. Pulling her mouth to mine, we shared the same air as I stared into her eyes. "Give me one more."

She shook her head. "I can't."

I pressed my forehead into hers. "Yes, you can. Come for me one more time, Vi. Come for me and I'll give you my come."

Reaching between our bodies, I found her clit and rolled my fingers over it three times to set off her biggest orgasm yet. She locked her limbs around me, holding me in place, and bit my lip as she came hard. I growled out her name and felt fire shooting down my spine and through my balls as I came hard in her. I could feel my come filling her, leaking out with how much there was, and more kept coming. Her core milked me until I had nothing left to give and even as I held her to my chest and stumbled back into one of Jack's office chairs, it still pulsed around my dick.

Collapsed in the chair, I held Violet to my chest and groaned into her hair. "Jesus. Are you okay?"

She panted against my neck and hugged me tight. "Better."

My mouth felt bruised and I felt like I'd just run a marathon, but I was flying high. I felt fucking great. "Sex has never felt like this, Vi. This shit is insane. I knew that first night we had something special."

"I felt it, too." Her lips brushed my neck as she spoke. "I figured it was just me being a virgin, though. After I didn't hear from you, I figured it was probably not as good for you guys."

"We almost didn't leave you to report to work. That's how amazing it was. We had to drag ourselves away. For the first time in our entire military careers, we didn't give a shit about work. You wrecked us." I ran my hands up and down her back, loving the feel of her smooth skin. "I'd almost managed to convince myself I'd imagined the magnitude of it when you showed up again."

She sat up and looked down at me with her breasts on full display and my cock still lodged inside her. Her skin was flushed and sweaty, but she'd never looked better. "What do you think it is? This thing between us, I mean."

I smiled slowly, giving her a look that said I knew exactly what it was between us. She just wasn't ready for that, yet. I didn't blame her. "Don't ask questions that you're not ready to have answered yet, Vi."

Her cheeks managed to flush even darker and she was quick to lean into me and kiss my bruised mouth. With her lips still grazing mine, she whispered. "I want to be ready. I'm just a coward sometimes."

I hugged her tight. "Bullshit. You're no coward. You're a lot of things, Violet, but I'm pretty sure a coward isn't something anyone would ever call you."

"Did you know it's not unusual for women to have multiple partners in Harmony Valley?"

"I'd heard of a few relationships with more than one man involved, yes." I searched her face. "Why?"

"Do you worry about people judging us?"

Laughing, I ran my hands through her hair and eased her back so I could see more of her. "Violet. Even if we lived in the middle of a town where no one had ever seen anything like what we have, I wouldn't give a shit. My feelings for you and for Forrest are bigger than what anyone could ever say or think. Here, though? No one bats an eye. If anything, I've been approached more since people started gossiping about us. Normally, people are intimidated by me, but now? Now, they just come up and start congratulating me and shit."

She gawked. "You're kidding."

I shook my head. "Nope. I miss the days when people avoided me."

"I'm torn between feeling horrified and amazed at the sweetness." Shaking her head, she finally looked around the office and stilled. "Whose office is this?"

I grinned. "Jack's."

"As in, the owner's?" Her face told me how much she

hated that idea.

"Yes. That very Jack. He owes me. The least he could do is lend me his office for a little while." I thought about how he'd used my room one night when we were younger and shuddered. "This doesn't put us anywhere close to even."

"I think I wrecked his desk." She pressed her face into my shoulder and sighed. "You make me lose control."

"I'll put his shit back on his desk. He'll be fine." I kissed the side of her head. "Come on. If I'm lucky, you'll let me walk you home."

She giggled softly. "I'll let you drive me to Margaret's to pick up Forrest."

"Even better." I stood us up, gently pulled out of her and placed her on her feet. Watching her clench her thighs together made me laugh as I fixed my clothes and grabbed her torn panties. "Problem?"

"You left a mess." She pulled her dress back over her breasts and shifted from foot to foot. "Seriously, Ben. I feel like if I move wrong, I'm going to leak your come all over this office floor."

I groaned and rubbed my hands down my face before handing her the panties to clean herself up with. "Even that wouldn't make me and Jack even. Any other time and I'd take my time cleaning you up, but I don't want to be late picking up Forrest."

"That's so sweet."

I realized she was serious and shook my head. "We've got to raise the bar for you, Vi."

CHAPTER 28
Violet

"How'd you manage to come alone to the bar, anyway? Normally, you're all three glued at the hip." I glanced over at Ben and felt a rush of endorphins. We were walking to Margaret's house because the weather was beautiful and I wasn't ready for our time alone to end yet.

"They both had to go into the office. One of our clients had a problem and it's a client they've both worked closely with." Ben squeezed my hand and smiled. "Unlucky bastards."

"Coco said you hired her when no one else would. She likes you guys." I stepped into his side as a cool breeze picked up. "Were you working with a client when you were gone? When I first got to town, I mean."

"Coco is a badass. Whoever didn't hire her is a fool. She's terrifying and I've seen her take down bigger men than me." He wrapped his arm around me and held me close. "We *were* working on a case when you got to town.

It took a month but they don't all take that long."

I frowned. "Do you guys leave for work all the time like that?"

Ben must've noticed the hesitation in my voice because he stopped and turned me to face him. "We don't have to do anything. We take the cases we want. We give the others to our employees. In the beginning, we took whatever case came our way, but that was before you and Forrest. We've already talked about it. We won't take a case that's going to take more than just a few days. We don't want to be gone that long anymore."

I nodded, feeling my chest loosen. "Okay. That's good to know."

He cupped my face in his big hands. "You and Forrest are our priority now, Violet. We'll show you."

A deep bark broke our focus and I looked up to see Captain pulling Mason towards us. General was farther behind with Justin. I grinned and absently rubbed my arm where it was still sore. Ben kissed me quickly and then gently tried to ease me behind him.

I scoffed and pushed past him so I could greet Captain with a hug and get his normal sloppy, wet kiss to my chest. I laughed and rubbed his ears while he panted happily. "How'd you find us? Huh? Are you a good search doggy? Yeah? Are you a good search doggy, Captain?"

Mason grunted. "He must've caught the scent of betrayal. Ben. Fancy seeing you here."

Ben grinned. "Suckers."

Justin and General joined us on the sidewalk and he scowled at Ben. "Dirty move, Benjamin. Sending us to the office so you could sneak away to be with Vi? Not fair, asshole."

I picked General up and cooed at him. "And look at you, little man. Aren't you so sweet? Being so good on your walkies! I'm so proud of you, buddy."

Mason growled. "Hello? I'm standing right here, woman."

Leaning into him after putting General down, I wrapped my arms around his chest and kissed him. Long and lingering, I didn't rush it. I tasted mint on his tongue and smiled as I pulled back. "Hi."

"Aw, hell." He pulled me into his arms and dipped me before kissing me deep. He made love to my mouth and only stood me back upright when a car horn went off in the distance.

I giggled breathlessly, and fanned myself. "Wow."

Not to be outdone, Justin pulled me into his arms and took his time tasting my mouth. By the time he really kissed me, I was clutching at his shoulders, desperate for more. When he finished, I stumbled a bit and Ben had to catch me.

"That's a much better greeting." Mason looked proud of himself as he watched me. "Judging by the marks on you, I guess Ben found a way to have his way with you."

Ben smacked Mason's arm. "A gentleman doesn't kiss and tell."

"We made a mess of Jack's office." I slapped my hands over my face and shook my head. "Why did I blurt that out?"

Another horn blaring jarred me out of our little group and I looked up to see the car that was honking was sitting at the stop sign across the road from us. The headlights made it impossible to see what kind of car it was, or who was in it, but it seemed like they were honking at us.

"Who is that?" Justin muttered under his breath as the three of them calmly positioned themselves in front of me.

I tried to move around them, but they were a human shield I couldn't bypass. "Guys, you don't need to block me from a honking hooligan."

A car door slammed and the sound of kitten heels running across pavement struck me. It was a familiar sound. Thanks to years of listening to my mother speed walk everywhere in her own kitten heels, I could identify the sound anywhere. I peeked around the guys and my heart stopped. Those kitten heels sounded so familiar for a reason. My mother was rushing towards us, a horrified look on her face.

"Violet! Violet, honey? What in the world is going on here?" Rose Channing, my mother, sounded about as happy as I felt in that moment. "Get out of my way, you three. Move!"

Ben's growl of a command came swift and sure, freezing my mother in her tracks. "Stay where you are. Come any closer and you'll end up on your ass, ma'am."

I pressed my face into Mason's back and squeezed my eyes shut. I didn't know what to say. I was panicking. I knew I didn't have a choice but to come out and face her, so I wedged my face between Mason and Ben to look at her. Clearing my throat with the subtlety of an earthquake, I forced a smile. "Hey, Mom."

The guys' heads snapped around to me. Justin choked out a surprised question. "This is your mother?"

Mom let out an indignant huff and crossed her arms. "Of course, I'm her mother. And who the hell are you? Why are you kissing my daughter in the street? What in the world is going on here?"

Dad had parked the car and was making his way over to join us. He stopped next to his wife and stood there stoically as Mom continued speaking.

"Where is Forrest? This is the kind of thing we were worried about with you moving away with him. You aren't responsible enough to raise a child without us. You should've left him with us. He would've been better off. Does he see this stuff? He's going to grow up and think this is normal, Violet. Good lord. I can't believe this."

Ben let out an angry laugh. "Forrest is right where he belongs. Same goes for Violet."

"Excuse me? Who are you and what do you know?" Mom inched closer. "That's my daughter and grandchild. You need to mind your own business."

"She *is* our business!" Mason raised his voice and then took a deep breath and tried again in a lower tone. "Violet is our business. So is Forrest. And you coming in hot like this, insulting Violet, is done."

"Watch it, young man." Dad actually raised his hand and shook his fist at Mason. "Don't talk to my wife like that."

Seeing things going poorly fast, I wedged my way out from behind the guys and pressed my hands against my stomach as nerves turned it jittery. "Mom. Dad. Stop. These are my...friends."

CHAPTER 29
Violet

"We're more than your friends, Vi." Ben gripped the back of my neck and squeezed gently.

I looked up at him and then over at Mason and Justin. They stared back at me expectantly; making it more than clear they weren't willing to pretend to be anything other than what they were. Swallowing the nerves fluttering in my throat, I forced my mouth to form words. "They're my... I'm with them."

"What the hell does that mean?" Dad looked back and forth between the four of us and scowled. "It better not mean what I think it means."

"Dad. I'm twenty-seven. I think we're past the stage where you threaten my boyfriends." I sighed. "We're together, I think. It's new."

Justin took my hand and nodded at me. "We're together."

"Oh, my god. This was all a mistake. Letting you bring

Forrest here was a terrible idea. Where is he? I need to see him and make sure he's okay." Mom shook her head at all of us and gripped my dad's arm. "I can't believe you're just…kissing multiple men in the street like it's normal, Violet. I didn't raise you to act like that."

Mason put his hands on his hips and grunted. "Forrest isn't your kid, ma'am. If you can't see that Vi is a great mom, that's a sign of a bigger issue in *you*. Violet is amazing with Forrest and he's a great little boy because of her. She's got support and family here now. If you can't treat her with respect, there won't be much use for you here. You'll find the entire town feels that way. Your daughter is a loved member of this community already. You and your husband are the only people taking issue with her, so again I say, the issue is with you."

I looked up at him with warmth blooming through my chest. I wasn't used to anyone standing up for me, especially to my parents. Back home in Kansas, there was a hierarchy around town and people didn't just go against it. My parents were respected in the community. At least they had been before I'd come home, uneducated and pregnant. Still, no one would've gone against them for me.

"Mason's right. Your daughter is home here. Forrest is home here. They're both safe and very well cared for. Everything we have, she has. If you came here to just criticize her, you should know she has three pitbulls in her corner now who won't let you. Respect your daughter or leave her alone." Ben ran his hand into my hair and tugged lightly. "Forrest is happy here. Violet made sure of that. And now the four of us will make sure of it together. You should be happy he's going to have an army behind him."

Mom gaped at me. "What the hell is going on, Violet?

You've been here for barely any time at all and it sounds like you're already playing house with these men."

I might've been in shock, but I felt like I was floating on cloud nine. Hearing them stick up for me and confirming they had every intention of taking care of me and Forrest was like sinking into a warm bath. My smile was probably silly considering the circumstances, but I was happy beyond belief. Looking back at my mother, I felt years of tension and stress slipping away. "They're Forrest's dads."

Both my parents looked confused. Mom narrowed her eyes at me. "What are you talking about?"

I straightened my shoulders and nodded. "I came here almost seven years ago. I met Mason, Justin, and Ben. They rescued me after my friends abandoned me at a bar. I got pregnant that night. We lost contact before I found out I was pregnant but when I moved here, we reconnected. Forrest doesn't know they're his fathers yet, but he already loves them. They're great men. He's lucky to have them."

Justin smiled down at me. "We're lucky to have him."

"You slept with all three of them?" Mom gasped and covered her mouth with her hands. "You don't mean…"

I groaned. "Mom! I do mean I slept with all three of them at the same time. I'm still doing it. I'm going to keep doing it, as long as it makes us happy."

"Which is forever." Mason crossed his arms over his chest. "Are you going to be nicer to your daughter?"

"This is… This is outrageous. Listen to yourself, Violet!" Mom turned towards Dad and tugged at his sleeve. "Make your daughter see reason, Steve!"

Dad raised his hands as he nodded at me. "What do

you want me to do? I've never been able to talk to her."

I took a deep breath and took a step closer to them. "Why'd you really come here?"

Mom's eyes filled with tears but she quickly looked away to hide them. "We're used to seeing Forrest more than this. We miss him."

"Then I'm glad you're here. If you just want to see Forrest and spend some time with him, that's great. He'd love it." I lowered my voice. "You're not allowed to make those little harsh criticisms you sometimes like to make of me, though. No more. I'm his mother and he doesn't need you polluting his head with your negative opinions of me. I'm sure he'll have plenty of his own when he hits his teenage years.

"I hope he doesn't make you feel the way you've made me feel. It's painful to have your own child turn against you." Mom withered in on herself and I would've felt terrible if I hadn't seen her act a hundred times before.

"I love you, Mom. I just can't live my life for you. You've disapproved of every choice I've ever made as an adult and you've made it clear to anyone and everyone who will listen. I'm tired of accepting that as what I deserve. I'm happy in Lilyfield. So is Forrest. He's making friends and setting down roots. Roots that I want, desperately." I gestured to the guys behind me. "They're his father. *We're* his parents. There is no *letting* me take him from you. I've raised him from the day he was born. The only thing I ever asked of you and Dad was a place to stay. You got to be grandparents back home because I did all the work. For you to come here and act like I've never been responsible enough to take care of Forrest is absolutely wrong. It's insulting as hell, too."

Dad looked down at his wife and wrapped his arm around her. When it looked like she was going to speak, he seemed to squeeze her tight. "You're right, Violet. This is none of our business. We should get to our motel and make sure we're checked in. We'd like to stay and spend some time with Forrest, if you'll allow us."

I exhaled heavily through my nose. "I would love for it to be your business. I'd love for you to stay and see Forrest, *and* me. It's your choice, though. I love you both. I work at the diner. You're more than welcome to stop by. Forrest will be excited to see you both, but I'll let you surprise him."

When neither of my parents said anything back to me, Ben growled and stepped forward. "For fuck's sake. Your daughter is practically begging you to be her parents and you can't think of a thing to say back to her. Shame on both of you. Get it together."

He wrapped his arm around me and tugged me down the street, away from my parents. I looked back and saw Dad was pulling Mom away, but she was glancing back at me, too. Our eyes met and I held my breath, waiting for her to say something, but she just turned back around and left.

I sagged against Ben's side. "Well, that could've gone better."

CHAPTER 30
Violet

That night, we picked up Forrest and the five of us crashed on the couches in the main house with the dogs. Forrest thought it was amazing, having a sleepover with the guys. I needed a bit of extra support after facing off with my parents. I'd never been so blunt with them and I knew that without the guys at my back, I would've continued to take their crap. It made me want to stick close to them, just in case my parents went on the offensive again.

Once my head hit the couch, I was out. If the guys thought I might be up for sneaking around in the middle of the night, they were sorely disappointed because I didn't move until an alarm went off the next morning. I jerked awake and looked up to see the guys shoving their shoes into the boots they'd kicked off the night before. They were moving faster than I'd ever seen them and just that sight gave me a spike of anxiety.

"What's going on?" I sat up, clutching a blanket to my

chest. "Is everything okay?"

Ben hurried over and kissed the top of my head. "Go back to sleep. We have a work thing."

I frowned at the spaces they'd occupied because they were gone just that fast. I heard a truck speeding away from the house a few seconds later. There was no way in hell I was going back to sleep after that. I grabbed my phone and saw that it wasn't even five o'clock yet.

Yawning, I looked over and saw Forrest had slept through their exit. I knew I couldn't just stare at the ceiling until it was time to wake him up, so I rose and quietly folded the blankets we'd used and rested them on the back of the couch. I straightened everything I could and then walked around the first floor, curious to see everything.

In a hallway towards the back of the house, a space no one would typically go, there were framed photos on the walls. The story of Mason, Ben, and Justin played out through the pictures and I followed along as best I could. I saw pictures of them as kids, all playing in a lake while several adults watched over them. I saw prom pictures of them looking awkward and lanky, their arms wrapped around each other's shoulders while their dates stood off to the side, making faces. There were pictures of them hugging their families as they wore military gear. There were even a few of them somewhere in a desert, looking sweaty and dirty, still with their arms around each other.

I followed their journey until the photos stopped with one of them outside of an office building. Justin held a key in the air and Mason looked like he was telling the contestants of a game show what they'd won. Ben stood in the middle, his face serious and his hands full of a case of beer. A sign behind them read, Harmony Valley Security.

They'd traveled the world through their service and they'd experienced so much more life than I had. For some reason, they still thought I was good enough.

I stood there for so long, staring at their life in pictures, that it was past time for me to wake Forrest up and get him ready for school. We both ended up rushing through getting ready and we both looked a little rough around the edges when we got to our destinations that morning. Forrest was still groggy as he went into the school and I felt like I was slowly melting into a lazy puddle when I went into *Doll's*.

Coco let me in and her face was pinched in a way that made me nervous. I'd never seen her show any sign of emotion, so her expression seemed a portent of something bad. She looked me over and nodded to the back. "You look as panicked as the rest."

I frowned but as soon as I was in the back room with the rest of the Dolls, I understood what Coco meant. The place was chaos. Women were all over the place, raising their voices and shouting at no one in particular. Margaret stood on top of a coffee table and pumped her fist in the air, riling everyone up.

"We're not putting up with this! He's gone too far this time!" Margaret looked at me and pumped her fist in my direction. "We're tired of people telling us what to do, aren't we?"

I stammered and saw everyone turn to face me. "I... Yes?"

"Mayor Stevens threatened to pull my business license! He threatened to shut me down permanently! He's power hungry. This battle has gone to his head! He's even wagered that whoever wins gets to set the new town motto!"

Everyone gasped and then started talking all at once. I just stood there and tried to imagine what the motto would end up being if either side won. Crazy, I was sure.

"He said he was going to pull my license for being a crazy woman! That fool."

I scoffed. "If that was reason enough to pull a business license, no one in this town would own a business! He can't do that to you."

Joanie had finally inched her way over to me and she slapped my arm. "Not nice! I'm not crazy."

I shrugged. "Are you sure?"

"We should march over to his office and give him a piece of our minds!" Brenda looked out the window and nodded to herself, pumping herself up. "Let's protest. I can make a few signs really fast."

Joanie shrugged. "As much as I don't want to admit it, Violet's right. If Mayor Stevens is going to start pulling business licenses for being crazy, we're all fucked."

I slowly grinned to myself. I'd gone to a few protests at college, but I had a feeling a protest in Lilyfield was going to be different. Sure enough, in half an hour, we were marching out of *Good, Clean Fun*, and across the street to city hall. Brenda and a few other women had made signs and they were hilarious.

Mayor Stevens is afraid of pussy...cats. Touch Good, Clean Fun and we'll touch you. You're going down, Mayor Stevens! If you mess with Margaret, we'll give you a real battle!

"Wow." I looked up at Joanie and motioned towards the signs. "They were ready for all of this, huh?"

She grinned. "The way I hear it, they control themselves much more these days. I think the use of cameras all over town really slowed down a lot of their stuff. After Sheriff Micheals arrested a couple of old ladies for vandalism, everyone realized he was serious. The illegal stuff slowed down after that."

Outside of city hall, we positioned ourselves and started marching back and forth. It felt like one of the silliest things I'd ever done, because I doubted anyone really thought Mayor Stevens would pull Margaret's business license, but we were all committed to the act.

Margaret pulled a megaphone out of her giant bag and turned it on with a squeal. Putting it to her mouth, she started chanting towards the front doors of the building. "Hey! Ho! Mayor Stevens' got to go! Hey! Ho! Tell that man he's just too low!"

I giggled as I bumped into Joanie and chanted along as best I could while falling apart in a fit of laughter. Billie held a sign in her hand and hiked it higher when she spotted us. Pointing up at it, she gave us a thumbs up and cackled. Her sign read, *This is my favorite picketing sign.*

My mood had shifted entirely thanks to the women of Lilyfield. I felt I could take on the day after going to a protest first thing in the morning. At least I did, until I happened to glance over and see my parents standing in front of the diner, staring at me and my rowdy group of bandits.

CHAPTER 31
Violet

"Everyone, run! He's got a hose!" Brenda screamed and pointed at where Mayor Stevens stood in front of city hall with a water hose kinked in his hands.

Joanie and I ran into each other in our panic and then we were all screaming as cold water blasted us. Well, to be fair, Mayor Steven's spray nozzle was set on shower, so the water wasn't all that terrible. None of us wanted to be wet, though, so we all cleared out of there as fast as we could. Joanie and I ran across the street together, damp and laughing like we were teenagers. Even though I knew my parents were waiting on me, I couldn't help the smile on my face. There was nowhere like Lilyfield.

Joanie cleared her throat when she saw who she thought were customers standing outside of *The One and Only*. She fought to keep a more demure smile on her mouth as she held open the door for my parents. "Welcome to *The One and Only*. Come on in and Violet here will get you taken care of."

I caught her hand and squeezed. "These are my parents, Joanie. Rose and Steve Channing. Mom, Dad, this is my boss and friend, Joanie Cartwright."

Chase stepped into the open door and looked at Joanie's damp state. "A word, Joanie?"

Joanie rolled her eyes. "And that's the man who *thinks* he's my boss. It's nice to meet you guys. Breakfast is on me."

"*Now*, Joanie." Chase stormed off and left Joanie mumbling about what she thought of him as she followed him.

I laughed awkwardly and gestured for my parents to go inside. "Well? Come on in and I can get you some coffee and something to eat."

Mom hesitated and looked up at my dad as she clutched her hands together. "Well, your father and I aren't staying for breakfast. We were up very early this morning and we took a drive to clear our minds. We got breakfast on the road."

I wrapped my arms around myself and waited for the verbal punches. "Okay."

"It's clear you've set up a life here already. You… You look very happy, Violet. You have friends and…family. I don't know what you ladies were protesting, but you looked like you were having so much fun." Mom sighed like she was struggling with how okay I was. "You were never happy in Kansas with us. Was that our fault? We were harsh. Maybe even judgmental."

I swallowed a lump of emotion and stepped closer to them so we weren't blocking the doorway. "I don't want to make you feel guilty. I wasn't happy in Kansas, but I could've changed things. I just didn't know how. Lilyfield gave me a place where I can be myself. No one expects anything of me here. I'm disappointing anyone. I'm so happy here and Forrest is, too."

"Do you think it would be okay if we stayed around for a while? We really do miss Forrest and we'd like to meet you as yourself and not someone we wanted you to be. We won't be perfect. I still don't understand being with three men, but if you can just give us a chance, we'll give them a chance."

I looked up at Dad. "You feel the same way?"

Mom sighed dramatically as he chuckled. She swatted him and reached for my hand. "Your Dad has been telling me for years that I'm pushing you away. He's over the moon he was right. We both want this. We both want to try to be better parents for you."

I searched both of their faces and then looked down at my feet. "You always get another chance with me. I love you both. Forrest loves you guys so much. I know he'd love having you closer."

Mom squeezed my hand. "And you?"

"If it's this version of you, I want you here."

She nodded. "Message received. Loud and clear. We'll try our hardest, Violet. It can be hard when you think you know what your child's life should look like to make them the happy. We clearly didn't know, though. We didn't have a single clue what you needed."

"I can't say I did either, for a while."

Dad yawned and then scoffed when both of us gave him disbelieving glances. "What? I didn't get much sleep. I'm tired."

"Why don't you guys go back to your motel and get

more rest? You can pick Forrest up from school at three and maybe we can have a family dinner tonight." I hoped I wasn't putting my foot in my mouth. "The guys, too."

After taking a deep breath, Mom nodded. "Okay. I'd like that. We got off on the wrong foot with your guys. It'll be nice to set things straight."

I laughed and pulled her in for a hug. "Aww, Mom. You don't have to fake anything. Your eye twitched when you said the word 'nice'. Don't strain yourself."

Dad laughed. "She's an easy read."

I hugged him next and then stepped back and took them in as a whole. They looked hopeful. It wasn't a look I recognized on them, but I liked it. "Dinner tonight then. I'll call and let the school know you'll be picking up Forrest today. There's only one elementary school. You can't miss it."

When I finally got behind the counter, Joanie was there, helping Jacob with a frown on her face. He looked as miserable as she did. I put on my apron and took note of all the customers before tapping Joanie out.

"I'm sorry about that, Joanie. You can go on back to your office now. I've got this."

She turned her back to Jacob and stared at the pie case with tears filling her eyes. "He makes me so angry, Violet. I can't go back there with him."

I inched closer and inconspicuously slipped her a napkin. "Say the word and I'll take a frying pan to his head."

She laughed even as tears streaked down her cheeks. "If I thought it would help, I'd do it myself. He's bringing in two of his investor buddies, Violet. He wants to try and make this place something it's not."

"Don't let him. This place is yours, Joanie. Fight him." I hugged her tight, surprising her. "Fight him and I'll help. We'll all help."

She took a slow, deep breath and nodded. "You're right. Okay. I'll do it."

"Just not tonight, because I invited my parents to have dinner with the three men I'm sleeping with." I ran my hands through my hair and laughed like I had a plan and wasn't freaking out. "But tomorrow? Tomorrow, I'll get my frying pan and I'll do whatever you need."

"Oh, god. Just worry about yourself for now. I need to think of a plan first. Something it sounds like you didn't do." She lifted her chin and turned her gaze towards her office. "Someone's sitting in my chair and I've got to kick them out of it so I can start planning."

I watched as she went marching off and almost felt sorry for Chase. He was about to get his ass handed to him. Before I could watch him tuck tail and run, though, Jacob coughed to get my attention and nudged his empty mug towards me.

"Can I get a refill or will your boyfriends threaten me over that, too?"

I shrugged and glanced over his shoulder. "I don't know, but we could ask them."

He swung his gaze around, but there was no one there. Looking back at me, he wagged his finger. "Why do I still like you?"

"I can't answer that, either."

CHAPTER 32
Violet

Thick arms wrapped around my waist from behind and Ben pressed a kiss to my neck. "Everything looks delicious, Vi. Consider me thoroughly impressed."

I leaned into his warmth and looked out the window over the sink to see Forrest playing with my parents in the yard. The dogs were with them and they all seemed to be having the time of their lives. "Thanks for letting me use the kitchen. And the dining room. And thanks for agreeing to have this dinner in the first place."

"Stop thanking me." He kissed along my neck to my shoulder. "Your parents said they're going to keep Forrest tonight."

My body flushed and I pressed my hips into him shamelessly. "I've missed you guys."

He slid his hand over my stomach and cupped my sex through my leggings. "We've missed you. Spread your legs for me, Vi."

I gripped the counter and did as he said, even as I told him it wasn't a good idea. "They're right out there, Ben. I don't want to get caught."

He pushed his hand into my leggings and panties. "We won't. I just want to help you relax."

I gasped as his rough fingers settled over my clit. "*Ben…*"

Making tight circles over the sensitive nub, he growled against my neck and pressed his hard length against my ass. When I slapped my hands over his arms and held onto him, he stroked me faster. "That's it, Vi. Come for me. This is an easy one. Later, I won't stop until you're begging."

I ducked my head and held my breath as I came. It wasn't one of the crazy orgasms they normally gave me, but it was still better than I ever did for myself. It was exactly what I needed.

Ben pulled his hand free and kissed the side of my head. "I can't wait to fuck you tonight."

I turned into his chest and smiled up at him. I felt much more relaxed and when I stretched taller to kiss him, I also felt happier. They hadn't come into the diner that day and I really had missed them. Running my hands through Ben's hair, I couldn't stop myself from saying the things on my mind. "It's pitiful I missed you guys today, isn't it?"

He shook his head. "No. I missed you."

"Was everything okay with work? You guys raced out of here and then never said anything about it." I watched as a part of his smile faded. "I'm sorry. I guess I shouldn't ask about it."

He gripped my chin and tilted my face up to his. "You

ask anything you want, Violet. Some things we won't be able to tell you, but it's dependent on the client. This morning was a government thing, so I can't tell you about it, but it should be okay."

I nodded like I understood. "Okay. As long as you guys are good, that's what matters."

"We're good. And everything you put together here looks good. I'm glad your parents decided to play nice."

I looked over my shoulder at them. "Me too. They seemed sincere. I hope it's real."

"They'd be crazy not to want to have a relationship with you, Vi. You're amazing." He nodded at the sight of them heading inside. "I'd better get rid of my erection. I don't think my second chance with them will go so well if I don't."

Laughing, I reached down and cupped him through his jeans. "Be nice to him. And tell him I'll see him later."

Ben groaned and disappeared just as my parents came in with Forrest. The dogs followed and General came right up to and took an extra wet lick along my chest.

Forrest laughed. "Mom! You got slimed!"

Mason and Justin walked in, their eyes on my slobber covered chest. Mason shook his head. "General strikes again."

I heard my parents and the guys talking while I hurried to the hallway bathroom to wash my chest and hands. When I got back, Forrest was regaling everyone with a story about his school day. Mason and Justin were leaning on the counter next to the sink and my parents were sitting on the other side of the island, their eyes going between the men and Forrest.

I walked over to sandwich myself between the guys and

smiled when they both moved closer to me. Glancing up at each of them, I felt my heart flutter.

Mason leaned in closer with a crooked smile stretching his lips. "What's that sweet look on your face about?"

I rested my hand on his stomach and shrugged. "Don't know."

He leaned in and kissed the tip of my nose. "Little liar."

Forrest came over and wrapped his arms around me. "Mom! Did you hear what I said? Bella is my girlfriend."

I completely forgot to play it cool. "What?! Girlfriend? My baby is too young to have a girlfriend! Oh, Forrest. You can't grow up on me."

He groaned when I hugged him tight and then wiggled away from me. "Mom! I'm not too young! I'm six!"

Real tears filled my eyes but I didn't want to seem like I was losing it, so I tried to laugh. "Oh, okay. Six is the new dating age? That's fine. That's totally cool."

Ben walked into the room and took one look at me. "Well, shit. What happened?"

My mother sounded like she was fighting to hold in a laugh. "Violet is watching her baby grow up and she's melting down over it."

Forrest groaned. "I'm not a baby."

Justin pulled me into his chest to support me and held me close. "Forrest, buddy, why don't we pretend like you're too young to date for a little while longer? For your mom."

Dad rolled his eyes and looked around the kitchen. "Please tell me someone has a beer for me."

Mason nodded. "I'll get a beer for everyone who isn't pretending to still be too young to date. I think we could all use one to take the edge off."

"She's crying over Forrest dating. When *she* was six, she cut off all her hair and glued it to our living room walls. She used to love scaring us, too. She would hide every chance she got and jump out when we were focused on something else. We'll probably both die ten years earlier than we should've because of her. But Forrest is dating and she can't handle that." Mom saw my shocked expression and laughed. "Sorry."

I put my hands on my hips and scoffed. "What the hell, Mom?"

Forrest looked between us and a sneaky smile slowly stretched across his face. "You liked scaring people? That sounds fun…"

CHAPTER 33
Violet

The table grew silent as everyone dug into their dinner. Mom and Dad sat across from Ben and Mason, I sat across from Forrest, and Mason sat at the head of the table. As someone's fork scraped across their plate, I glanced up and saw Mom studying Mason. My stomach clenched with nerves as I watched her put her fork down.

"I didn't like the way things went last night." Her tone was calm, but I wasn't sure I could trust it.

"Mom…" I glanced at Forrest, sitting next to Mason, and shook my head. "Maybe we could talk about this later."

She picked up her glass of water and took a long sip. "Honey?"

I cringed. "Yes?"

"Relax." She smiled at how floored I looked before turning her gaze back to Mason. "I hated it. I realize now that I hated it so much because you were defending Violet from me, the way I should've been defending her from others all this time. It was hard to swallow that awful pill. You did what I couldn't, or wouldn't. All three of you did. Without hesitation, you were all three ready to fight for my daughter."

Mason swallowed the bite he was chewing and sat back in his chair. "Ma'am. We've gone to war for beliefs that weren't our own. Imagine what we'd do for a woman we believe in whole-heartedly."

Tears filled my eyes as his words sank in. I sniffed and tried to hide them, but Forrest called me out.

"Why are you crying, Mommy?" He walked around the table and climbed into my lap, forgetting his earlier declaration that he wasn't anywhere near a baby.

I held him closer and rested my chin on top of his head so I could meet Mason's gaze. "Mason said something really sweet, baby, and it made me happy. That's all."

"You cried because you're happy?" He climbed down and went back to his chair. "You're silly, Mommy."

"Damn. I really wish I'd been the one to say that." Justin grinned sheepishly at me. "Is it too late for me to take credit for the emotion behind it?"

Dad elbowed Mom and nodded at me. "Are you going to start wanting more men around so you get doted on like this?"

Before Mom could reply, the same alarm that had gone off that morning went off again. The energy in the room changed instantly as the guys shoved away from the table. I looked up at them and felt the evening crashing and burning. They each already looked miles away as they silently communicated with each other.

"What's happening?" Mom looked at me with concern

coloring her expression.

Justin squeezed my shoulder as he backed away. "Work emergency. We'll be back."

Ben kissed the top of my head and Mason pressed a hurried kiss to my cheek before they vanished out the front door. Once again, the sound of their truck racing away followed shortly after.

I looked back at my parents and my shoulders slumped when I saw how much their happy expressions had dampened. Feeling the need to excuse their abrupt exit, I forced a smile. "They own a security company. Sometimes they have emergencies and have to go help."

"Oh." Mom looked around the dining room and pursed her lips. "Okay."

I didn't like that she was seeing flaws in the picture. I didn't like that I felt like maybe there were flaws, too. It made me speak out of turn. "Oh? What, Mom? What do you have to say about it?"

Dad frowned at me and shook his head. "Forrest and I are going to go play with the dogs. You and your mother can talk. Try to remember your manners, Violet."

I rested my elbows on the table and braced my chin on my fists. I hated the feelings churning in my stomach. I hated I was worried about the guys leaving and I hated that Mom could see it.

She took a deep breath as she pushed her plate away from her. "Violet... I'm not trying to attack you or what you have here."

"Please, don't."

"Do they have to rush away like that for work often?" She saw my mouth turn down and rushed on. "I'm not trying to be critical, Violet. I watched your face when that alarm went off and you looked sad. Are they able to be here as much as you need them to be?"

I stood up and started clearing the table. "This is only the second time they've had to rush away since we reconnected."

"That's not bad, then. You've been here for weeks."

I stopped with my hands full of plates and looked down at my feet. "The first two weeks I was here, they were out of town for work."

"Oh, Violet." Mom rushed after me into the kitchen and cornered me at the sink. "They seem great, they really do. You need someone who can be here for you and Forrest. Do you think they can do that? I'm not saying they can't be. I'm just...asking."

I stacked the dishes next to the sink and wrapped my arms around myself. "They don't have to take on the cases that are farther away. As the bosses, they get to choose which ones to take on. Ben was telling me last night that they've spoken about it and they don't want to leave on long cases anymore. Not since me and Forrest are here."

"That's great, honey. Or maybe if they do have to take on one of the bigger cases, one of them could stay behind with you. There has to be some benefit to having three men." Her voice trailed off. "You don't seem like you think it's great, Violet."

I forced a laugh and shook my head. "I lost them once. Their job scares me, I guess. Seeing them rush away, it worries me. It's not just me I have to think about. What if we do this and then Forrest watches his dads run out all the time? What if they don't cut back on the long trips? As much as I care about them already, I don't know them well enough to know they won't leave."

"Well, honey, you never know anyone well enough to know anything one hundred percent." She grabbed my hands and tucked them both against her chest. "I don't want my daughter waiting around on men all the time. Personally, I would prefer you find a man, or men, who are here for you and Forrest. You deserve that. I can tell you care about them, though. Maybe just slow things down and be careful."

I felt her hesitating and closed my eyes. "Just say the rest, Mom."

"No matter what you think or want, Violet, you have to tell Forrest they're his dads. You can't make that choice for him, or them, out of fear. He deserves a dad. Or dads, as it may be." She squeezed my hands and then pulled me in for a hug. "He loves them. He talks about them nonstop. He even told your father he wishes they were his dads. Honey, you're not doing yourself any favors by trying to control this."

My chest tightened. "He said that? He said that he wishes they were his dads?"

She nodded. "Your dad said Forrest looked so hopeful it took everything in him not to blurt it out right then and there. We won't do that, of course. It's not our place. But you need to tell him."

"I'm so glad this night was so light and easy and that I don't have anything serious to spend my night losing sleep over." I looked out the window and saw General take Dad's legs out from under him. Smiling, I gestured at the window. "We should go save him. I'll clean up after you guys leave."

CHAPTER 34
Justin

I swore as Mason parked on the street in front of our house. Violet was already dressed for work and getting in her car. When she saw us, she hesitated before getting out and standing next to her open door with her arms crossed. Mason shut the truck off and rubbed his hands over his face. Ben took a deep breath. I swore again. We were all fucking exhausted. Some prick of a senator's son had gotten himself kidnapped by a rebel group in some backwoods part of the world and we'd been up all night, gathering intel and setting up calls with old buddies from the service. We needed eyes and ears near the rebel force as soon as possible. Before Violet and Forrest, we would've been wheels up the moment we got the job. Sending other people in our place wasn't easy.

"She's pissed." Mason shoved his door open and glanced back at me. "I hope she knocks me out so I can have an excuse to sleep for a few hours."

I met him at the front of the truck and stretched to

crack my back. "Being a boyfriend is hard."

Ben pushed past us and growled. "I'm too tired for you two right now."

Violet kept her arms crossed as we closed the gap between us. Her lips looked red and raw, like she'd been chewing on them. She had dark circles under her eyes, too. It looked like she'd slept about as much as we had.

Ben gripped the back of her neck and pulled her into his chest. "You can hug me back or we can stay just like this all goddamn day."

"Ben." I leaned against the car and positioned myself in the way of her escape. "You're upset with us, Vi?"

She heaved a giant sigh before wrapping her arms around Ben. When he let her go, she hugged Mason and then turned to me. Moving to hug me, she gasped as I grabbed her hips and pulled her mouth to mine. I kissed her until her hesitant mouth became hungry and I was in the middle of considering making her late for work when she pulled away suddenly and frowned at me. "I *am* upset."

I licked her taste from my lips and nodded. "Tell us."

She tucked her hair behind her ears and took a few seconds before meeting my gaze. "I'm not upset *at* you. I'm just…disappointed, I guess. I was looking forward to last night."

Ben growled under his breath. "I was, too, Vi. It was a work thing we had to handle so we could get back here to you. We did it as fast as we could."

Her cheeks heated. "I'm not… I'm not suggesting you guys were wrong for handling your work commitments."

"Then what are you suggesting?" Tired Ben wasn't exactly going to win any awards for mincing words.

"My mom said something after you guys left last night.

She's worried about me being with someone who can't be here for me and Forrest." She looked down at her feet and her voice grew quieter. "It worries me, too."

Anger boiled up my throat. I hated that her mom didn't trust us to take care of her daughter and grandson. To hear that Violet didn't trust we could take care of her was salt in the wound. "It was one night, Violet."

She nodded and sent her hair flying in her face. She didn't bother pushing it back. "Of course. Let's just forget it."

"No. If you don't trust us, we need to know." I looked to Ben and Mason and saw them giving me glances that said to chill out.

"It's not that I don't trust you. I'm just scared of falling for men who aren't home. It's not fair for me to ask you to give up your career. If your career keeps you gone for weeks at a time, though, I'm just not sure I want that life for me and Forrest." She rubbed her arms. "Waiting around to see when, or if, you guys come home, doesn't sound like a peaceful life."

"Violet, we've turned down a couple of longer jobs already. I told you we aren't going to leave like that anymore. None of us can stand the idea of leaving you and Forrest here alone." Ben brushed her hair back and cupped her face. "We don't have to take a single job we don't want to take and none of us want to take a long one. We want to be here. We wanted to be here last night. It would've been nice to convince your parents to give us their blessing. Instead, your mom has more reasons not to like us now."

I held her hips and pressed my face into her shoulder. "You can't give up on us before you even give us a chance,

Vi."

She took a shuddering breath and held it. After too long for my comfort, she blew it out. "I've never done this stuff before. It's all scary. I'm not giving up. I'm just…moving with caution."

Mason stretched and yawned. "I don't mean to be an asshole, but you're ours. You can move however you want because at the end of the day, you're going to be right here with us. We're going to do right by you, Violet. Go ahead and give it up because we're going to prove to you we're everything you need."

Violet was quiet for a moment and then she giggled. "Okay, then."

Ben looked at me and rolled his eyes. "I guess that was all it took? I could've done that."

"Oh. Mom said something else last night."

I groaned. "What now?"

"She said I needed to tell Forrest that you guys are his dads. The faster, the better." She glanced back at me and raised her eyebrows. "You're lucky you're cute even when you're unfairly sassy."

My heart thumped harder. "Are you going to tell him?"

"I was hoping we could do something tonight."

The three of us were suddenly wide awake and over the moon. Ben's smile was as big as I'd ever seen it. "Tonight? Hell, yes! I'll get balloons."

"Balloons?" Violet laughed full out and shook her head. "I don't think we need balloons."

"Well, I'm getting balloons." He picked her up and spun her around. "Thank you, Vi."

Mason looked at his watch and pulled out his phone. "I know a cake lady. I'm getting a cake."

"I'll get pizza." I thought about what all I wanted Forrest to have. "And toys."

"Okay, okay. There's no need to go nuts. He's going to be so happy just to know that you're his fathers. Nothing else will matter." She backed towards her open door. "I have to go to work now. Are you guys sure tonight will work? If you're still busy with work, just say so."

I shook my head even as Ben spoke. "Tonight is perfect. We'll take care of everything. You and Forrest can just show up."

"Let us take care of you two." I kissed her red lips and breathed in the fresh scent of her. "Let us in, Vi. We're begging here."

She nodded. "I'm trying."

CHAPTER 35
Violet

The day had stretched on and on. My nerves were on high alert, despite the guys' reassurances. I was terrified of telling Forrest. I had to do it and I'd loved seeing how happy it made the guys, but I was scared of what it would mean for me and Forrest. He'd officially no longer be just mine.

By the time the day ended, I was a sweaty mess, despite the dropping temperatures. I'd spilled two cups of coffee on myself and even managed to lean right onto a slice of pie. I was stained and gross. I didn't want to face anyone in the state I was in so I had my parents pick up Forrest and I rushed home to take a long shower.

More nerves plagued me as I dried off. I felt an incessant need to look nice for telling my son who his dads were. I changed clothes a dozen times and took my time curling my hair and putting on makeup like I hadn't in years. When I left to pick up Forrest, I was in a short dress and boots. The dress had long sleeves, but it did nothing to combat the cold. I was freezing and incredibly overdressed for a pizza party.

That thought was cemented when Forrest ran out of my parent's motel room and stopped dead in his tracks when he saw me. His eyes widened and he stammered for a moment before finding his words. "Are you going to church, Mommy?"

I met my mom's eyes over his head and blushed. "No, baby. We're just going to dinner with Justin, Ben, and Mason."

"And General and Captain?"

Mom gave me a thumbs up as I backed away with Forrest. "Call me later."

"You'll be asleep."

She laughed. "I'm staying up for this."

I groaned when my nerves flamed even higher. "Great."

In the car on the way home, Forrest peppered me with questions. "What are we doing? What's for dinner? Can I have ice cream tonight? Grandpa let me have ice cream last night."

I reached over and held his hand. "You can have ice cream. You can have whatever you want, Forrest. I love you."

"I love you, too, Mommy. What if I want a dinosaur?"

"I hope you decide you want it to be small and plastic. I'm not sure I'm ready to run from a real dinosaur." I parked by the garage way too soon and looked over at Forrest. "You know I love you no matter what, right?"

He nodded and pushed the door open. "Come on, Mommy. I want to see the guys!"

They were waiting for us on the front porch. They

didn't appear to have the same nerves I did. They seemed cooler and calmer than ever. They greeted Forrest with big hugs and shot me appreciative glances. It was Mason who spoke up first. "I can't not say something. You look stunning, Vi."

I curtsied and then rolled my eyes at myself. I was nervous and it was making me weird. "Should we go in for dinner?"

Justin nodded and held his hand out for Forrest's. "We have a surprise for you."

Forrest cheered and jumped up and down. "I love surprises!"

Ben caught my hand and held me back on the porch with him. After Forrest was inside, he pulled me closer and smiled down at me. "You're the most beautiful woman I've ever seen, Vi. You also look sick with nerves."

I leaned into his chest and let him hold me. "I'm scared. I keep trying to think of the perfect time to tell him, but there is no perfect time. Besides now. The sooner, the better. He needs to know."

"Thank you for giving us this, Vi. It means everything to us. It makes *us* that much more real. After this, maybe you'll officially move in and we can fuck you to sleep every night."

I tried to fight the smile stretching my lips but it was useless. "So romantic."

Forrest's voice called me from inside. "Mom! Come, look!"

I narrowed my eyes at Ben. "What did you do?"

He grinned. "It's a big occasion. It deserved a big to-do."

I hurried into the house and saw there were balloons

everywhere. There were also toys everywhere. Forrest was on the floor, in the middle of a stack of blocks. His smile when he looked up at me was huge. I went to my knees next to him and ruffled his hair. "Wow! Look at this stuff! Someone must really love you."

"We have pizza, cake, and ice cream, too!" Mason's voice was shaky and I realized we were all in uncharted territory. It felt like a band-aid situation. We just had to rip it off.

Forrest pumped his fist in the air. "Best day ever!"

I swallowed a thick lump of emotion and cupped his small face in my hands. Stroking my thumbs over his cheeks, I smiled a watery smile at him. "Hey, kid. We have something to tell you."

Justin dropped the bag he was carrying and sank onto the couch behind Forrest. "We're all pretty excited about it."

With all three of the guys around us, I took a deep breath and brushed Forrest's hair out of his face. "I know you've wondered why you don't have a da—"

The alarm sounded again. It pierced through the silence in the house and shattered whatever peace we'd had. The guys scrambled to gather their things but they stopped beside us for long enough to talk that time.

Justin looked angry as he ran his hands through his hair. "I'm so sorry, Vi. Just… Give us a little bit. We'll be back as soon as we can and we can tell him then."

Mason nodded. "We'll hurry back. Don't eat all the pizza without us."

I kept my head down, afraid I'd burst into tears if I looked at any of them for too long. I fumbled with a block and had to clear my throat so I could speak clearly. "Sure.

Be careful."

Ben kissed the top of my head the way he seemed to always do when leaving. "Hold down the fort for a bit, Vi. We'll be right back."

Forrest happily played with his blocks, unaware of the tension. "Can we play when you get back?"

Justin chuckled. "Of course, buddy. Keep your mom company for us."

I didn't look up again until I heard their truck drive away. My feelings were flayed open all around me and it was all I could do to not burst into tears.

"What were you going to tell me, Mommy?"

I stood up and dusted off my butt. "Are you hungry? Do you want some pizza?"

"I want to wait on Justin and Mason and Ben."

Forcing a smile, I looked at my son finally and nodded down at him He looked nervous and I knew it was my fault so I sat down on the couch and held up a game controller. "Should we play something while we wait? I bet I can kick your butt."

His smile returned full force and he hurried over to me. "No way, Mom! You're a girl!"

I scoffed. "I have so much to teach you, kid."

Glancing up at the door, I told myself to relax and focus on Forrest. The guys said they'd be back, so they'd be back. I just had to trust them.

CHAPTER 36
Violet

I jerked awake after a fitful night of sleep and sat up gasping for breath. I'd been having a nightmare but I couldn't remember what it was about. I could still feel the panic and stumbled to the bathroom to splash water on my face.

After waiting hours at the main house the night before, I'd finally given up on the guys coming back in a timely manner. I'd cleaned up the house as best as I could and carried Forrest back to our house. He'd passed out without eating dinner and I was worried about him so I went to check on him but he wasn't in his bed.

"Forrest?" I moved through the rest of our home and couldn't find him anywhere. With my heart beating painfully fast, I ran outside and down the stairs. I heard sobbing as soon as I turned the corner of the garage and could see the main house. "Forrest?!"

He was sitting on the front porch steps, openly sobbing. His little body shook and he had snot running from his nose he didn't even notice.

I ran to him and my brain tried to think of scenarios for why he was crying like he was. I didn't see any wounds, but I couldn't be sure. I'd assumed that since he was outside, the guys had come home, but he was all alone. I sat next to him on the porch and pulled him into my lap. "What's wrong, baby? What happened?"

He spilled his guts through a stuffy nose and broken sobs. "I saw them outside and I wanted to play. I remembered to put on my shoes and when I got downstairs, they were getting in their truck. They didn't hear me, Mom, and they just left me."

Anger clogged my throat but I held it in. "I'm sorry, baby. They didn't hear or see you. If that did, they would've stopped for you. You know that?"

"They had bags. Are you moving? Are they leaving me?"

I held him tighter. "No, Forrest. They aren't leaving you. This is their home and you're their…friend. They must've gone on a trip for work. I'm so sorry this happened, though, baby. I know it hurt your feelings. They'll be back and you can talk to them about it. Okay?"

He wiped his nose on my shirt and nodded. "I just wanted to see them and play with my toys with them."

I stroked his hair back from his face and worked hard to keep my face neutral. "I know, Forrest. I miss them, too. As soon as they're back, you can challenge them to whatever fun games you want."

He just shrugged continued to look heartbroken.

"Why don't we go back to our house? I'm starving. How about you? I'll make breakfast." I held my breath and hoped pancakes helped some. "I'll add chocolate chips to your pancakes if you want."

"I'm not hungry, Mom."

I led him back upstairs, planning on finding my phone and ripping the guys a new one as soon as I could. Especially when Forrest went back to his bed and pulled his blanket over his head. "I'm going to make pancakes just in case you change your mind, buddy."

He didn't reply but I hadn't expected him to. He was shutting down.

I grabbed my phone from my bedside table and rushed into the bathroom. I tried calling each of them, just to be sent to voicemail. I called Ben last so it was his voicemail that got the message. "He watched you guys drive away. He ran down to catch you and when you didn't hear him, he watched you leave. I found him crying on your front steps, sobbing. You can't do that to him. You can't break his heart. It's not fair."

I hung up and sat on the toilet. I felt like crying for myself, too. I wasn't sure I could handle their job. I was just running my thumbs over my screen when I noticed I had a text. Opening it didn't make me feel any better.

An emergency case came up that we have to take care of. We'll be back in two days, at the most. We boarded General and Captain.

How...efficient. I put my phone down and leaned forward to rest my elbows on my knees. It was an emotionless message from men who weren't ready to commit to relationships. With me, or Forrest. They'd left in the middle of us telling him they're his fathers and left a cold text as a goodbye? After making it so clear that they *chose* the cases they took on, it was clear they'd *chosen* to leave on a longer trip. They'd chosen a trip over telling Forrest.

SUMMER HAZE

We hadn't even told Forrest they were his fathers yet, and they were already hurting him. I didn't want a life of pain and disappointment for Forrest. He deserved more than that.

I hid in the bathroom and cried. I ached for Forrest, but I also ached for me. I cared about them. I wanted them. I wanted them to be the men they promised they'd be.

I tried to shake myself out of my funk and ended up making the saddest pancakes ever. I picked at them while Forrest wouldn't take a single bite. We were both miserable and there was a giant hole in our lives that was gaping open. It turned out there was a very large downside to being connected to three men in the way we were. Their presence was that much larger and so easily felt. And missed.

That night when I put Forrest to bed and crawled into my own feeling defeated and down, I pulled out my phone and reread their message over and over again. Nothing changed, but I was quickly slipping into pathetic territory. Before I could change my mind, I sent a text to all three of their phones.

Be safe.

CHAPTER 37
Violet

"Violet?" Jenny's voice was strained as she tried once more to get my attention. "Are you there?"

I shook myself out of the shocked silence I'd been in and cleared my throat. "I'm here. Um… I'm sorry, Jenny. Can you repeat what you said? I'm not sure I heard you correctly."

"I know this is unexpected. Believe me when I say that I was shocked." She sounded like she would've rather been saying anything else to anyone else. "Forrest acted so out of character today so I sent him to the nurse's office to see if he was running a fever. He lashed out at other students, was mean to even his best friends in class, and refused to participate in any of the activities. I've never seen him like that, and after the last incident, I pulled him aside to see if there was anything else going on… He wouldn't say a word to me, Violet."

I was horrified to hear my son was acting like that, but

I knew exactly what was wrong. "I'm so sorry, Jenny."

"Is everything okay? I didn't send him out today after the way Principal Boyd acted towards him last time, but if he's like this again tomorrow, I won't have a choice. He made Sophie cry today."

"I… I'm just so sorry. Um. I don't know what all to say. Forrest got really attached to Ben, Justin, and Mason. He's crazy about them. They went out of town for work a few days ago and he's not taking it very well." Understatement of the year. "They were only supposed to be gone two days, but it's been almost a week."

"Oh, Violet, I'm sorry." Her tone made it clear that she felt bad for me.

That tone got under my skin in a bad way. What was she sorry for? Did she think the guys had left me? Did she think they were hurt somewhere? Or worse? Why did she feel bad for me? Everything was fine. "I'll talk to Forrest."

"If you need a break, Violet, I could watch him." She was being so kind and trying her best to help, but she was ruining my very fragile state of delusion.

"I'm okay. Thanks for calling." I hung up and walked back out into the diner, set on keeping myself together. I had to.

I'd barely been back on the floor for five minutes when Joanie walked in from running an errand and shook her head at me. I forced a smile while sliding a customer a refill of their coffee. It'd been a rough week for me, too, and the cracks were starting to show. While Forrest was lashing out in anger, I was just…scared. Not knowing if the guys were safe, or even alive, was eating away at me. I flashed back and forth between grief and anger, but the anger never lasted. I cried myself to sleep every night and I was starting to feel like I was losing it.

"You're done." Joanie walked up to me and untied my apron. "You need to go home and get some sleep. Have your parents watch Forrest and just rest. You look like you're barely standing, Vi."

Tears filled my eyes and I shook my head. "I'm okay. I'm absolutely fine. I can do this."

"Violet, go home. You—"

"I said I'm fine!" I realized I'd shouted and covered my mouth with my hand. "I'm so sorry, Joanie. I—"

"Hush. You're not going to hurt my feelings by raising your voice at me, Vi. I'm not changing my mind about this, though. You need to go home and rest."

I nodded my head too fast and a wave of dizziness washed over me. I braced myself on the back of one of the booths. "Okay. I'll go."

"Are you okay?" Chase came out of the back and must've caught my dizzy spell.

I cleared my throat. "Yeah. Yes. I must be feeling a little under the weather."

"I'm sending her home." Joanie put her hand to my forehead and frowned. "When's the last time you ate?"

I glanced out the window to avoid her gaze. I couldn't remember. Lunch the day before? I wasn't sure. As I was opening my mouth to answer I spotted a familiar face across the street. Angel. I grabbed my purse from behind the counter and raced out of the diner. I cut across the empty street and chased after Angel.

She must've heard me huffing and stumbling because she swung around to face me with a stern look on her pretty face. It didn't relax when she saw me. In fact, her eyebrows pinched together tighter and her lips turned down even more.

I stopped right in front of her. "I'm not sure if you remember me, but I'm a friend of—"

"I know who you are." She took a deep breath and shook her head. "Whatever questions you're about to ask me, don't."

Tingles erupted over my entire body like millions of tiny needles jabbing me with adrenaline. "I just need to know that they're safe. I haven't heard from them in a week and they told me—"

"I get it. It's not fun being the one left countryside. I can't tell you shit, though. I don't know shit."

"They're not in the country?"

She swore. "Look. Whatever they're working on is top secret. I'm sure they're fine. They're the best there is."

I stumbled back a step.

"The guys won't tell you this because they clearly like you, but being a partner to someone in this field is miserable and lonely. I don't think I saw the guys more than seven times last year and I work for them. You look like you're seconds from breaking. If you can't handle the not knowing, maybe you should get out before things get too messy." She gently squeezed my arm. "I'm sorry. As one of the only women in this field around here, I've always been passed off on the wives and shit during parties and things. I've heard a lot of horror stories over the years."

"Okay." I turned around without another word and walked towards my car.

A thousand thoughts were racing through my mind. I was feeling what 'not knowing' did. I could see it with Forrest. Neither of us were cut out for it. The guys weren't going to change. We would never be able to harden ourselves against their absence. Not for a long time, anyway, and not without a lot of pain.

Piper Young, one of the high school teachers, opened the door of her car right next to mine and it hit mine. She swore and got out, her face going red. When she noticed it was me, she let out a giant exhale, like she was glad to see me. "This is your car, right?"

I nodded. "It's fine. It's the least of my worries."

"No, no. I scratched your door. I'm just racing around right now during my lunch break. Did you know the school only gives us twenty minutes? Twenty minutes to get over here, make fifty copies to hang around town, and then get back to school." Freezing, Piper's eyes widened, and she giggled. "Unless you want to rent the slightly above crappy apartment over the pharmacy, which would save me all this hassle."

"How much?" The words were out of my mouth before I could even make a conscious decision, but I knew. As soon as I asked, I knew if I could afford the apartment, I was going to take it. I needed to distance myself from the guys. I couldn't do that from their garage.

"Oh? Oh, wow. I thought for sure that wasn't going anywhere." She looked at the paper in her hand. "My aunt is moving away to live on a cruise ship with her new boyfriend for a while and it's her apartment. She has rent listed at…"

I held my breath.

"Oh, here it is. Rent's only three hundred a month." She shrugged. "What do you think?"

"I'll take it."

CHAPTER 38
Ben

Three weeks later

"Still no answer." The words tasted foul in my mouth. We'd been stateside for six hours and we'd been taking turns calling Violet the entire time, but she wasn't answering. I squeezed the phone in my hand and took a deep breath. "She's pissed."

Justin rubbed his face and I winced at the deep bruises around his eyes. "We don't even know what a pissed off Violet looks like. This mission couldn't have come a few months down the road? At least then we'd know what we were walking into. Obviously, she's not a big talker when pissed. Is she going to throw things? Scream?"

"We told her two days and vanished for a fucking month." Mason shook his head and cracked his neck. "We'll be lucky if she doesn't hate us."

"Not a fucking option." I ground my teeth and looked around Senator Jacob's private plane. We'd saved his asshole kid. The kid had managed to get involved with a gang of mercenaries. Hunting them down had been a long and painful process. We all had wounds and battle scars, but we'd bypassed doing anything other than getting on the plane and leaving. We were all disgusting, but it didn't matter.

"That time, she just ignored the call right away." Justin growled and threw his phone down on the couch next to him. "I've got a bad feeling."

"Fuck off." Mason narrowed his eyes at Justin and then dialed again. Someone picked up after a moment and when I leaned forward, Mason shook his head. "Hey, Angel."

I absently listened to his conversation until he mentioned Violet's name.

"Have you been down to the diner? I was just wondering if you'd seen Violet… Where…Just on the street?" He frowned. "Oh. Yeah, okay. No, that's fine… Alright. We'll check in later tomorrow, probably."

As soon as he hung up his phone, we were on top of him. Justin bounced his foot. "Well?"

"Angel said Violet chased her down in the street three weeks ago and asked if we were safe." He rubbed his jaw. "Angel wouldn't tell her anything. She said Violet didn't look great, though."

I growled and dialed her number again. That time the call went straight to voicemail. "She's turned her phone off. How fucking long until we land?"

"Forty-two minutes." Mason tipped his head back and closed his eyes. "I hope Forrest is okay."

"He will be. We'll fix this." Justin sighed. "I think I'm done. We're getting too old for this shit anyway. Now, we've broken a promise to Violet within a day of making it. I'm done traveling."

I pressed my palms into my eyes. "If we want a chance, we have to be done. We have to make sure the structure is in place so we're free of this. I'll never feel bad about saving someone, but not at the risk of losing our family."

When we landed at the small airstrip behind the office, it didn't take us any time to shove off and get to Mason's truck. Normally we would've gone in and done a debrief with the team, but we had more important things to worry about.

The closer we got to our house, the deeper the pit in the bottom of my stomach grew. I knew something wasn't right. I'd learned to hone and trust my gut after so many years in the field, but I was praying it was wrong. It seemed like we were each feeling that bad feeling by the time Mason parked in the driveway because we all charged upstairs to the house above the garage.

I knocked hard and waited to hear the sound of life inside, but there was only silence and then rolling thunder in the sky behind us. I tapped in the code to unlock the door and stepped in to find nothing. My mind couldn't make sense of what I was seeing. There was no sign that Violet and Forrest had ever existed in the space. Scrubbed clean, none of the personality remained.

I went from room to room and by the time I checked the bathroom, I knew it. She was gone.

"There's a note!" Mason called us into the kitchen where there was an envelope with our name on it sitting on the counter. Mason held the paper from inside the envelope in his hand. "She left."

Justin grabbed the paper and read the words out loud. "I couldn't stay here, not knowing. Before you come find us, maybe think about whether you're ready to be fathers, or not."

"That's all it says?" Anger burned its way from the bottom of my stomach, all the way through me. "Two fucking lines for her Dear John letter?"

"We had to save someone's fucking kid across the world. It's not like we were off partying. Why would she question if we're ready to be fathers? We were here. We were trying." Mason shook his head. "Fuck this. We're going to find her and she's going to hear us out before she tries to leave us with a two-sentence letter."

I dialed Margaret and the second she picked up, I knew she knew where Violet was. "Where is she?"

"I do everything to help you boys out and you go and shit the bed like this? If I didn't know your hearts, I'd tell you to fuck yourself." She hesitated. "Since I've been watching the poor thing struggle for the last month, maybe I'll still tell you to fuck yourself."

"Tell me to fuck myself and then give me her address, Margaret. We need to see her."

"God, you men. All of you are drama queens." She huffed. "She's living in the apartment over the pharmacy. If you're going, you'd better be back for good."

CHAPTER 39
Violet

The last month had been hell. I'd tried my best to just keep moving forward, but things were crumbling. Forrest hated me. He believed I took his friends away. He was still getting in trouble at school, Mom and Dad were at their wit's end with him, and just getting him to school was torture for both of us. All my years of trying so hard to be a calm and kind parent had been shattered. It was impossible to be calm and kind to a kid who acted like you were the devil. He hated everything. The new apartment, Mom and Dad's new house, literally everything.

I felt like I'd gone through a month of the most intense emotional bootcamp but I hadn't come out the other side stronger. I just felt broken. I was lonely and I spent most of my time going back and forth between missing the guys, hating them, and thinking the worst until I was physically ill. I barely got any sleep and I felt like I was crashing.

Hearing they were home and safe had been a relief. On

the other hand, I was terrified of running into them. Was I supposed to see them around town and not shatter? I didn't know if I could stand under their intense gazes and not fall apart. Even seeing their names on my phone had gutted me. I'd locked myself in the bathroom and sobbed, thankful they were okay, but after that, I didn't know what to feel.

Forrest was in the bedroom, throwing stuffed animals from one side of the room to the other. He wasn't speaking to me. It would've been a nice reprieve from him telling me he hated me but the constant sound of stuffed animals hitting the walls was starting to wear on me.

Jenny was supposed to stop by with a few books she suggested might help Forrest, so when there was a knock at the door, I assumed it was her and pulled it open. It wasn't Jenny. It was the guys.

They weren't fully themselves, though. They were covered in bruises and cuts and their clothes were stained brown with what had to be dried blood. They had thick beards and smelled like sweat and fuel. Seeing them look so rough scared me and when I heard Forrest coming out of the bedroom, I panicked. He couldn't see them like this. I slipped out of the apartment and shut the door behind me.

Tears burned my eyes and escaped down my cheeks. I couldn't help it. They looked like they'd been through hell. "You can't be here."

Ben reacted like I'd slapped him. A flash of pain crossed his face before it hardened into anger. "What the fuck are you doing?"

I wiped my eyes and catalogued their injuries. "Forrest can't see you like this."

"We're not going until you talk to us. You don't get to leave us with a 'Dear John' letter, Violet." Ben stepped closer and braced his hand on the door next to my head. "I'm sorry it happened like it did. Shit went bad and we couldn't get back. We did the job and now we're home. We're not leaving again."

I wrapped my arms around myself. "I don't believe you. How can I?"

"Violet, please. Just sit down and talk this out with us. We care about you and we know you care about us." Justin blew out a deep breath. "We messed up, but it was to save a kid's life. We weren't out partying."

"This is just making the pain last longer." I shook my head. "It doesn't matter if I care about you. Keeping you in my life isn't good for me. I can't be the woman who stays at home while you put your life at risk in another country. I don't want to be that woman. This month was the hardest month of my life. Harder even than having Forrest on my own, and being the unwed pregnant woman in a town full of judgmental people. Not knowing if you guys were alive... Not knowing if I was going to have to tell my son the men he cares about aren't coming back. You guys don't understand what it's like to have to look at your child and tell him you don't know when the people he loves are coming back. You didn't even say goodbye."

"I'm going to need you to be stronger." Ben lowered his face so we were eye to eye. "If you care about us at all, you have to be."

I pushed him away from me. "Be stronger? That's what you have to say to me? Do you want to know how strong I've been? My son has spent the last month lashing out at everyone around him. He's told me he hates me no less than two times a day. The little boy who I used to be able to talk through his feelings? Gone. He thinks I somehow got rid of you and he blames me for you being gone. He's been kicked out of school multiple times for bullying other students and my parents can't even talk with him. He hates *me* because *you* didn't keep your promise.

"I've barely slept in a month because every time I try to go to sleep, I think about you three being dead somewhere and me never finding out what happened to you. This town kept moving, but life for Forrest and I just stopped. As much as I think it's amazing you saved someone's kid, I have to think about my child. I have to think about the damage this is doing to him. I don't want a life of watching you leave. And that's what it'll be. You told me you choose your own assignments and you don't take ones you don't want to. You wanted to go across the world for this assignment. You left on the night we were going to tell Forrest."

"He's not just your child, Violet." Mason's voice was low and I ignored him.

"Your own employee warned me away from you guys. She knows you'll never change. I'll always be waiting. I'll always be comforting Forrest after you leave again. And one day, maybe you won't come back. I think it's better if we don't tell him…" I stared down at my feet and held myself tighter as I realized I was shaking. "I don't want him to grow up like this."

"That's bullshit and you know it, Vi. We're telling him. You're just going to have to trust us. We aren't leaving like that again." Justin growled out his words, anger coloring his cheeks.

"I don't believe you!" I cried harder and grabbed the

doorknob. "I don't believe you and I don't even know if you believe yourself."

"We're his fathers!" Ben's shout made me flinch and I saw his face twist in regret right away. "I'm sorry. Fuck, Violet. Just come home. Please. Let's just talk about this after we've all slept and calmed down."

The door behind me opened and I nearly stumbled into the apartment. I caught myself but when I saw Forrest rushing out to run into the guys' arms, I almost wished I'd fallen and knocked myself out. "Forrest! Back inside."

"You're my Dads?!" He clung to them. "I heard you! You're my Dads!"

Ben met my hurt gaze and held out his hands. "I'm sorry, Vi. I didn't mean to—"

"Forrest, get back inside. I need to finish talking to the guys." I watched him ignore me and felt myself free-falling without any chance of regaining control. "Forrest!"

"Leave me alone!" Forrest turned around and shouted at me. "You made them go away but they're back! I want to go with them!"

"Forrest, baby, I love you. Please listen to me."

"I hate you! You can't make them leave again!"

"Forrest!" Justin's voice was sharp. "Don't talk to your mom like that. She didn't make us leave. We had to go to work. I'm sorry we've been gone so long. Your mom didn't do anything wrong, though, and you need to be nice to her."

I curled in on myself, more defeated than I'd ever been. I quickly tried to suck up my tears and force a smile. I wasn't doing anything good by keeping Forrest locked in the apartment with me. He hated me and he didn't want anything to do with me. "Go and pack what you need to stay the night, Forrest."

"Violet…" Ben reached for me but I flinched away from his touch. "Goddammit, Violet, we don't want to take him from you. Come with us."

"We can work out custody. Right now, um, it seems like he doesn't want to be here with me. If one of you could drop him off at my parents' tomorrow evening, that would be good."

"Violet, please." Mason's soft plea nearly broke me. "Don't do this. We're not leaving again. We fucked up. Multiple times. Don't give up on us. What we have is special."

I wiped my eyes again as Forrest came out with his backpack stuffed full. I knelt down and held my arms out for a hug, but he shook his head. I closed my eyes, desperately trying to hold back the tears at his rejection. I looked back at him with a watery smile. "Did you get everything you need to stay the night, baby?"

"Violet, just come with us." Ben pleaded. "We want you there."

Ignoring him, I stood up and nodded at Forrest. "It'll be just like when you spend the night with Grandma and Grandpa. Have fun, okay? I love you, Forrest."

He tugged on Justin's hand. "Let's go!"

"If he needs anything, my parents have multiples of everything. Mom left their numbers on your fridge when she was there." My mind raced. "My car's unlocked so you can just take his booster seat. He doesn't want to ride in it but he has to for now."

"It's not supposed to be like this, Vi." Mason reached for me but let his hand fall when I shied away. "We want you with us. We never wanted to take him from you. You have to know that."

"Have fun, Forrest. Be good for them. Mommy loves you so much." I shut the door and as fast as I could, ran to the other side of the apartment so when I broke down, they wouldn't hear it.

CHAPTER 40
Mason

The sound of her sobbing carried through the thick apartment door and ripped my heart to pieces. It was the sound of a wounded animal. She was so hurt, so fucking miserable, but still pretending to be okay with sending Forrest off with us. I couldn't just leave her like that. *We* did that to her and walking away with Forrest wasn't something I could do.

"I'm not leaving her." I looked at my two best friends, the men who'd been as close as brothers for most of my life. "And if you can, you're not the men I thought you were."

Without waiting to see what they would do, I opened the door she hadn't bothered locking and followed the sound of her cries. She was curled up on the kitchen floor, as far away from the front door as she could possibly get. I sat down next to her and pulled her into my lap. All the fight had gone out of her and when I wrapped my arms around her, she clung to me.

She was taking in heaving breaths but still, it was as though there wasn't enough oxygen in the room to calm her. Her body trembled in my arms and I could feel she was panicking.

I took slow, even breaths, letting her chest rise and fall with mine. "Breathe for me, Vi. In and out. Just like that."

She turned to get even closer to me and it seemed like nothing was enough until she was straddling me and I was wrapped so tightly around her she couldn't move. Then, she spoke in a quiet voice. "I'm scared."

"What are you scared of?"

She shivered and her teeth even chattered. "I've already lost you guys once. It was horrible but I didn't know you then like I know you now. This month was a snapshot of what it would be like and I'm not strong enough. I can't do it. I wasn't even mentally here enough to talk to Forrest and make him understand it wasn't my fault. I was lost."

"Violet, I'll never go on another assignment overseas. I won't even take one in the states if it's going to be longer than a day. Seeing you hurting… I don't ever want to chance being the reason for your pain again. I'm so fucking sorry we did this job. We didn't know it was going to be what it ended up being. I won't take that chance again. I'm sorry, Vi. All I wanted when we got back stateside, was to see you and Forrest. I wanted to make sure you'd been okay without us. Knowing that you weren't… It's never going to happen again."

She looked up at me with her eyes wide and tears brimming. "I thought you were dead. I tried talking to Angel and I even called your office. I just wanted to know if you were okay. I was terrified. You didn't say goodbye before you left and if something happened to you… No one would tell me anything. I'd spend the rest of my life waiting on you to come home. I've already spent the last seven years waiting to find you guys again. There's no one else for me. That's scary. I don't want to fight. I love you and I'm afraid even if you think right now, you'll never leave on a job, you could change your mind in the future."

I sucked in a sharp breath and caught her cheek in my hand. "What did you say?"

"I said a lot of stuff."

"You said you love me."

She shrugged. "So?"

"If you think you're getting rid of me after telling me you love me, you're wrong. I've never been loved by the woman I desperately want to love me. I'm not giving it up because I fucking love you, Vi."

She pressed her face against my neck and I could feel her smiling. That smile faded fast, though. "Forrest hates me."

She couldn't see what I could. Just outside of her front door, Justin and Ben were sitting with Forrest and there were some stern, fatherly looks happening. I was glad they were talking to him because I wanted to shake some sense into him for treating his mother like he had.

"No, he doesn't. The way you two normally communicate, is amazing. You're the best mom I've ever known and you've done it alone for his entire life. This seems like the first big upset he's been through and he had a lot of anger with no direction for it. Unfortunately, it looks like he's going to take after his fathers with that." I stroked the hair out of her face and kissed her forehead. "He knew he could take his anger out on you and you weren't going anywhere. That won't be something we let happen, though. You're his mother. We're not taking him from you."

"But he wants—"

"You're a package deal. I love you, Violet. I want to love you in our home and spend every night with you. I'm not going home without you." I leaned back so I could look her in the eye and let her know how serious I was. "You're scared. I get that. I'm scared, too. I've never felt this way before. I've never been a father before. There's always the chance you grow tired of us. Or that Forrest realizes we're nothing compared to you."

"He loves you guys so much. He—" She blinked up at me with those green eyes rimmed in red. "You love me."

"Did you not hear me earlier? I love you. I think I loved you the moment I saw you all those years ago." I cupped her cheeks in my hands. "You're ours. More than that, though, we're yours."

"It didn't... I'm just... I heard you but it didn't register. You love me." She chewed on her lip and studied my face. "And I love you."

I nodded. "So, can you see how silly it would be, not to be together?"

Her lip trembled and she clenched my shirt in her hands. "What if you resent me for needing you to give up this part of your life? What if you end up hating me?"

"Vi, I've been going out on assignments for too long. I've been saving people and bringing them home to their loved ones with nothing to come home to myself. I'm sure there are people who would call me selfish but I'd give this career up a million times over for a chance with you." I stroked her cheeks and ran my hands down her shoulders and arms until I could unclench her fingers from my shirt and hold them. "I'm sorry about this last job. We still have work to do in restructuring the company so we aren't necessary. Until we get it perfect, we'll push the big cases through to friends who can handle them."

"So, it won't be perfect?"

I frowned and shook my head. "I'll be honest with you, even though all I want to do is tell you exactly what you need to hear to get you home with us. It won't be perfect at first. I *can* promise you we won't get sucked into another case like this one, but there might be a job or two that does require an overnight or even two. We built the company around ourselves and it'll take some time to fix that. You can come with us, though. To the office, not on trips. You're not getting anywhere near any kind of possible danger. And by that I mean you're not even allowed near a vehicle without a top safety rating."

She took a deep breath and when she met my gaze, she was smiling. "That answer is much better than an empty promise it'll all be perfect."

I released the own breath I hadn't realized I'd been holding. "You'll come home with us?"

She lifted a single shoulder. "I don't know if that's what's best for Forrest right now. He deserves time with just his dads."

"Violet…"

"He needs you guys. Whatever he's going through, he needs you and not me." She leaned into me and sniffled. "It hurts. I knew things would change, but I assumed I'd always be his world, the way he is mine. I can't fight this, though. I won't."

CHAPTER 41
Justin

Mason walked out of the apartment with an unreadable expression on his face. He walked around Forrest on the steps and turned to face our son once he was a few stairs below and could look at Forrest on his level. "Are you proud of how you treated your mom?"

Forrest tucked his chin to his chest, showing he could be just as stubborn as the three of us. He hadn't budged an inch with me and Ben.

"I know you're only six, Forrest, but you're still responsible for your actions. You made your mom cry."

Forrest cut him off. "Mom cries every night."

I bent forward like he'd slammed his fist into my ribs. It hurt to hear what we'd done to her.

"Yeah. We did that. We made her cry because we left and she didn't know if we were safe. You were scared, too, weren't you?" Mason braced his hand on the railing. "We have to be responsible for what we did, too. We messed up. So now we don't get what we want. You made her cry, too. When we get home, you're grounded, Forrest."

Ben shifted and I could tell we both felt uncomfortable with the idea of punishing Forrest so fast. He'd just learned we were his fathers. He was going to hate us.

Forrest stuck out his bottom lip. "Mom never grounds me."

"Because she's a really good mom and you were always kind to her. She didn't need to ground you. You haven't been kind to her lately, though, have you? You've been mean to your mom and that's not okay." Mason softened his tone but it looked like he was struggling. "Forrest, we love you. You're our son and we'll always be here for you. We're so happy we found you. I love you mom, too. I don't like seeing her upset. We both have to be better at not hurting her."

His little shoulders finally sank. "She wouldn't tell me where you were. She made us move."

Ben cleared his throat. "That was our fault. We didn't tell her where we were going, so she didn't know."

I knelt beside him. "She moved here because she was so hurt. Your mom didn't do anything wrong. You owe her a huge apology."

"Why didn't you tell her where you were?"

Mason sighed. "It was a secret. For our job."

"Mom didn't make you leave?" His little lip trembled.

"No. She tried to make us come back. That's why she's upset with us now. She didn't think it was fair for us to leave you like that. She was right, too. Your mom is a great woman, Forrest. She's nice and pretty and smart. She would never do anything to hurt you." I ruffled his hair and looked up at Mason. "We all owe your mom a giant apology. Then maybe she'll want to move back to our house."

Mason rolled his lips between his teeth. "She wants us to spend time with Forrest. Without her."

My stomach sank. "Is she sure?"

"She isn't budging." He ran his hands through his hair and looked back down at Forrest. "When we get home, we're not playing with any of those new toys. We're going straight to bed. You're grounded until tomorrow night."

Instead of pouting, Forrest nodded. "Okay."

"You're going to apologize to your mom, too."

"Can she come?"

Mason looked away and took a few deep breaths before looking back at Forrest. "She wants you to have time to be with us."

Big tears filled his eyes. "I'm sorry."

Picking him up, Mason held him close. "Your mom will forgive you. She'll forgive us, too."

I hoped.

It took forever to get Forrest into bed that night. He was upset and it was clear he wanted his mom, but he wouldn't say it. We talked more about how he treated his mom and by the time he fell asleep, he was ready to find her and apologize big time. He'd also sworn he'd never do anything like it again, but all knew that was a pipedream. He'd hit his teenage years and become a serious pain in the butt, just like everyone else, eventually.

After he was asleep, I met Ben and Mason in the living room with a beer. Sitting across from them, I groaned as my muscles ached. "I don't remember homecomings being so painful."

Ben stretched his legs out. "Well, I've been dying to

know what you talked about with Violet."

Mason rubbed his hands over his face. "If I never see her cry like that again, it'll be too soon. We hurt her. More than we were willing to acknowledge."

I drained my beer. "Spit it out."

"She loves us. She talked to Angel, who we owe a big conversation with, and she tried calling the office. She thought we were dead." He shook his head. "She's scared of what losing us would do to her."

Ben sighed. "I was an asshole. I just couldn't handle the idea of her shutting down on us. I was panicking about losing her and I treated her poorly. Then I outed the news to Forrest before she was ready."

"We were all assholes. We promised we wouldn't leave her like that and before the words even left our mouths, we did it for a month. Why should she trust us? Because we have major fucking chemistry? Because we tell her she has to? We fucking took her son." Mason stood up and paced behind the couch. "I'll never not see the pain on her face when she handed him off to us. That woman is too good for us."

I rubbed my jaw. "We haven't made things easy for her."

Mason scowled. "She's the best mother any of us have ever seen and we made her son treat her like shit. She's home alone right now, without him, and you heard Forrest. She cries every night."

"Why couldn't she just come with us?" I felt like throwing up. "None of us wants to take him from her."

"Even though she looked like it was ripping her to shreds, she wanted to give him time alone with us. She thinks he needs us and doesn't want to get in the way."

Mason looked like he was speeding towards an explosion. "I'm not going overseas for another rescue. I don't fucking care."

"None of us are. We'll take care of it." Ben rested his head back on the couch and blew out a deep sigh. "This isn't how I thought this night would end."

I studied Mason. "She said she loves us?"

He stopped pacing to smirk at me. "She said she loves *me*."

"I'm going to fucking bed." Ben stood up and was almost out of the room when he spun around. "If she loves you, then she loves all of us. That's a given."

"I don't know. She didn't mention either one of you."

I could tell they were heading for a fight so I moved between them. "We've already had enough of a hard time explaining our bruises and shit to Forrest. New ones can't happen."

CHAPTER 42
Violet

"Turns out that coward Mayor Stevens had to have an emergency colonoscopy. He's saying he won't be able to prepare for the battle so we have to push it back. I told him women have been getting things stuck up their butts for thousands of years and it's never slowed us down but that didn't stop him." Margaret crossed her arms over her chest and looked around at all the Dolls. "It's fine. It just gives us more time to prepare. Because of his postponement, I made him increase the bet. Winner takes all."

I looked over at Joanie and then to my other side at Billie. "What the hell is all?"

Joanie shuddered. "After all the butt talk, I'm terrified to ask."

We didn't need to wait long, though. Brenda appeared at Margaret's side with a poster. She turned it around to face us and we all just stared at it in silence. There was no way...

"That's right. If the women win the First Annual Battle of the Sexes, we win bragging rights, the right to choose the new town motto, and I will be mayor until the men can beat us in battle." Margaret grinned like she'd eaten the cat *and* the canary. "Our shops will be safe and when I'm mayor, this town will go pink for women's month. We're going to rule this town!"

Everyone seemed excited about it and they cheered along with Margaret, but I wasn't feeling it. I was sure it would be great if we won, but I couldn't make myself care that afternoon. I'd made it through my first night without Forrest and I hadn't slept at all. It was somehow different from the times he stayed with my parents.

"The new battle date will be decided at next week's town meeting. Be there! We also propose our battle ideas that night. This should be fun. I can't wait to see Mayor Steven's face when we announce that one of the battles will be pin the vibrator on the clit." Maraget clapped her hands together and then focused on me. "Alright, now I've got a little birdie to interrogate. Remember, the samples of the new peach lube are by the door. Grab them and go nuts."

"I've got a toy boyfriend who just loves peach." Billie grinned. "I'll see you ladies later."

I inched towards the door but Joanie hooked my arm and pulled me down on the couch with her. She smiled at me and reached up to tap the bags under my eyes. "I wouldn't normally subject you to Margaret's torture when you're clearly barely hanging on by a thread, but I think you need this."

I needed nothing more than to go home and pass out. Since Joanie had become obsessed with making sure I was okay, I knew I wasn't moving, though. "I'm fine."

Margaret pulled a pink fuzzy ottoman closer and sat in front of me. "That's a lie and we all know it. Everyone with eyes can see you're miserable. The guys called me demanding to know where you were last night. I expected to see you sleepless and ruffled today, but this isn't from sex. This is from sadness. What happened?"

I inspected my hands in my lap. "They came. We talked. Forrest made it clear he wanted to go with them. I let him."

Joanie squeezed my arm. "Oh, Vi. Didn't they apologize?"

I nodded. "Yeah. They were upset and didn't want to take Forrest from me but Ben accidentally spilled the beans they're his fathers and there was no stopping that train. Forrest wasn't coming back into the apartment with me without me forcing him. I didn't want to do that."

"Wait. So they apologized?" Margaret tapped her fingers on her knees. "Why didn't you leave with them? Especially since Forrest did?"

I took a deep breath and stared across the room at nothing. "They apologized. They were angry at me for leaving their house, though, so we fought a little. Then Forrest was there, announcing he hates me, and I just…gave up. Mason came in and we talked a little more, but I still don't know."

"What don't you know?" Margaret reached over and took my hands. "Honey, you love them. Everyone can see it."

I nodded. "I know. I love them more than I ever thought I could love someone who isn't Forrest. I miss them so much."

"Well, what's the problem?" Joanie turned to face me. "I must be missing something."

I sank back into the couch and stared down at where Margaret was grasping my hands. "I'm scared. I don't know if I can live through a repeat of this last month again."

"Let me let you in on a little secret. Whether or not you deny yourself the love of these men, that fear doesn't go anywhere. Love is fucking scary. Yeah, Ben, Mason, and Justin have jobs that are more dangerous than the normal Joe, but you would be scared to lose anyone you love as much as you love them. That's what it's like when you give your heart away." Letting go of my hands to pat my knees, Margaret stood up and wagged her finger at me. "You're no coward, Violet."

I turned to Joanie after Margaret walked away and scoffed. "Even though she said I'm no coward, I feel like she just called me a coward. That was the vibe, right?"

"Yeah." Joanie laughed and pulled me in for a hug. "You got a second chance with the loves of your life, Vi. They're the fathers of your son. Life, or Margaret, brought you back together again and you'd be a fool to let it slip away. They're crazy about you and Forrest. If fear's the only thing holding you back, let it fucking go."

I looked around the room and blew out a deep sigh. "Think Margaret will become mayor?"

Joanie snorted. "Hell, yeah. Then I think I may need to move. She's scary with power."

"What about you and Chase?"

Her head whipped around to face me. "There is no me and Chase."

"So, I'm the only one not allowed to be a coward?" I

raised my eyebrows at her. "I've seen the way he looks at you. There's chemistry between you two."

Standing up, Joanie pulled me to my feet and we walked out together, both of us stewing over our own stuff. Finally, she looked at me and frowned. "It's never going to happen with Chase."

"What if I said the same about my guys?"

"You'd be a liar. You just called them *yours*." She pulled me into a tight hug and then patted my cheeks. "You love them and they love you. Give them a chance."

I felt a wave of nausea and held still until it passed. "I feel sick at the idea of taking chances right now."

"Yeah, you just went green. Are you okay?"

I nodded. "Yeah, I'm fine. I don't handle big emotional dilemmas very well. You should've seen me after I found out I was pregnant with Forrest. I lost fifteen pounds through the first few months of pregnancy."

She laughed. "And you're sure you're not pregnant now?"

"I'm not. I…" When was my last period? I started to count backwards, but I couldn't remember having a period since arriving in Lilyfield. Another wave of nausea crashed over me and there was no stopping me that time. I doubled over and threw up right there in the middle of town.

CHAPTER 43
Violet

"Where are you, Violet? It's late and the guys stopped by to drop off Forrest, but Forrest either wants to see you or go back with the guys. He's still being a bit of a turd." Mom's voice was muffled through my phone's speaker, but I understood what she was saying. Her tone said it all. I should've been at her house hours ago.

I stared down at the pregnancy test in my hand and spoke through a husky voice. "Um… I had to pick something up at CVS and the closest one was forty minutes away. I just lost track of time."

"What did you need at CVS? You live above a pharmacy." She sounded even more worried. "What's going on, Violet? You don't sound right."

I cleared my throat and shoved the test back in the box. "I'm coming home now. I'm sorry about running late. Forrest can go with the guys if he wants to. Just tell him I love him, please."

"No, no, no. I don't like the way you sound." Mom sounded like she was running a marathon with the way she was speaking. "I've got her on the phone but she doesn't sound right. I'm worried something's wrong."

"Mom!" I threw the test on the passenger seat and pulled out of the parking lot. "I'm on my way right now!"

There was a lot of shuffling sounds coming through the phone and then Ben's deep voice was in the car with me. "Where are you, Vi?"

"Leaving CVS now. There's no reason for anyone to freak out." I thought about that pregnancy test. There was definitely reason to freak out. I was pregnant. I just wasn't sure I wanted to shout it out over the phone.

"Are you okay to drive?"

"Yes! I haven't been drinking, Ben. Jeez. I just went for a drive to get something and now I'm coming back." I swallowed a wave of nerves and then decided I needed time before I told them anything. "Forrest wants to go home with you guys and that's okay with me."

"Fuck that. It takes forty-two minutes to get here from that CVS, Violet. If you're not here in forty-two minutes, we're coming looking for you. We'll be here waiting."

I groaned when I realized he'd hung up on me. I knew that if I didn't go to my parents' they really would come looking for me. I didn't want to cause a scene so I just bit my tongue and drove straight to my there. Everyone was in the yard when I pulled in, which made me feel like a teenager who'd been out past her curfew. Even General and Captain were there. At least they ran to greet me with happiness. Captain even climbed into the car and refused to get out.

I left the giant dog in my car and wrapped my arms

around myself. No one made a move towards me, so I felt painfully awkward as I inched closer. My chest gave a tight squeeze at seeing the guys, but I forced myself to stay strong.

Mom looked me over from the porch and sighed. "I was worried something happened. You're never late."

"I just lost track of time. I'm sorry I was late." I looked around for Forrest and frowned when I didn't see him. "Where's Forrest?"

"He's waiting inside." Mason stepped closer. "We thought it would be better if we talked first."

My stomach churned and I swallowed down the need to vomit again. "What is this? An intervention? Guys, I'm fine. I'm not good at drinking. I don't do drugs. Smoking makes me want to gag. I don't gamble or have a sex addiction. What's the intervention for?"

"It's not an intervention, smart ass." Justin rolled his eyes at me. "It's us using every weapon in our arsenal to make you come home with us."

Mom nodded and moved down the steps. "They're right. You should go home with them, Vi. You were so miserable without them. You love them and they're offering you everything you've ever wanted. Take it."

"I thought you weren't on their side after their disappearing act."

She shrugged. "I got to talk to them. They love you, Vi. They love you so much that I don't understand it at times. They love the stubborn parts of you I want to strangle, and the sweet parts of you, you hide deep down. That's special. You don't find that every day."

"The concept as a whole makes me want to bleach my brain, honey, but they love you and you love them. That doesn't seem complicated to me." Dad smiled. "Forrest loves them. And we talked about them going away for business. Things are changing. You have to trust them."

I turned my gaze on the guys and shook my head. "You somehow managed to get my parents to fight your battles for you?"

Mason smiled. "You can't shame us. We have no shame when it comes to you, Violet. We love you."

I gritted my teeth. "Everyone thinks I should just forget all these fears I have and run back to you guys."

Ben nodded. "Everyone seems pretty smart."

"Can you promise me right now, in front of my parents, that you'll never disappear for a month again?" I pressed my hand over my stomach, thinking about the life growing inside me. "I've already been a single parent. If I'm going to have to deal with sharing a bathroom with three men, I want to know I'll never be a single mother again."

Justin grinned. "You will never be a single mother again. Not to a child, not to a dog, not to a fucking fish, Vi. We promise you, we will never disappear for a month again. We don't ever want to leave you."

"Do you promise you'll always be safe at work? You'll do everything you can to make it home to us?"

Mason nodded. "I've never been more motivated to get home, Vi. You're everything to us. You and Forrest are our world. We mean that."

"We want to take care of you and Forrest. We fucked up with that job and we deserved you leaving us. Even waiting less than an hour for you to get here, was torture tonight, so I can only imagine what we put you through. Let us make it up to you." Ben inched closer. "Let us spend forever making it up to you."

I wiped my eyes and swallowed around the lump in my throat. I was just opening my mouth to give in when General dropped something at Ben's feet and then flopped onto his back to roll around. My eyes dropped to the piece of plastic just as everyone else's did. The positive pregnancy test. General had just ratted me out to everyone.

"Are you…pregnant?" Ben's voice was thick with emotion as he picked up the stick. "This is yours, correct? Are you pregnant, Violet?"

Mom let out a soft cry. "Violet?!"

I nodded once. "I just found out."

"How accurate is this?" Ben flipped the stick over and growled. "How accurate, Violet?"

I tried to grab the stick from him but he caught my arm and pulled me into his chest. I felt my body react instantly to being close to his again. "I peed on that, Ben. Drop it."

"I don't give two flying fucks if you peed on it, Vi. You could piss on me right now and I wouldn't give a shit. We're going to buy more of these things." He shoved the test in his pocket and then picked me up. "Forrest stays with Grandma and Grandpa."

Mom clapped her hands. "This is just so exciting!"

I grunted when Ben gripped my ass tight and marched towards his truck. "Wait! I didn't agree to any of this."

Mason let out a bark of laughter. "Oh, sweetheart, that ship has sailed. You were already ours but we were trying to be patient. This changes everything, though. You're not getting rid of us."

Forrest ran out the front door and cried when he saw me. "Mom!"

Without me having to ask, Ben put me down. I

dropped to my knees and a second later, Forrest barreled into me, knocking me over. I hugged him tight and stroked his hair out of his face. "Oh, baby. Don't cry. Mommy's here. I love you, Forrest. I love you so much."

"I'm sorry, Mommy. I was bad to you. I love you and you're the best mom." Giant tears rolled down his cheeks as he held me around my neck in a way that a week earlier, I would've thought he was trying to strangle me.

"We all make mistakes, Forrest. It's okay. All that matters is that we apologize and move forward. You've gone through a lot of changes lately, baby. It makes sense you're having a lot of big feelings. I am, too. We're okay, though." I rocked him back and forth and glanced up to see Mom watching me with tears streaming down her cheeks.

"Sometimes we're not the nicest to the people we love. Your mom's right, Forrest. We just have to say we're sorry and do better." Mom cupped my face and smiled. "I'm sorry. I'm glad you didn't take after me. You're a wonderful mother, Violet."

CHAPTER 44
Violet

"Back again?" The cashier at CVS smirked at me when I walked in. "If you want my number—"

Ben's growl cut off whatever else the guy was going to say. Like a pack of deadly wolves, the guys moved with me as I made my way to the pregnancy tests. They were practically circling me and if the store had been busier, I feel like they would've kicked people out.

Standing in front of the shelves full of tests, I repeated the same mental song and dance I had earlier. It was harder with the guys watching me. Their impatience radiated off of them in waves. They had gone into a weird state of focus since seeing the pregnancy test General dropped.

"Fuck it." Mason just started grabbing one of each test. "I don't want to rush you, Vi, but I'm dying here."

"Mason! We don't need all of them!" I started trying to take them from him and put them back, but then they were all clattering to the floor and Mason was crashing his mouth to mine.

He backed me into the other side of the aisle and I gasped when he cupped my ass and lifted me so I wrapped my legs around his waist. His mouth was just as focused as the rest of their actions and his tongue tangled with mine in purposeful strokes that made me think of what he wanted to do to me. When I moaned into the kiss, he pulled back and growled. "Someone buy those. I'm taking Violet to the truck."

I buried my face in his shoulder as he carried me out. "I can walk, you know?"

"Don't care." He opened the back door of the truck and climbed in with me still in his arms. I straddled him and he cupped my breasts together and rubbed his face against them. He sucked my nipple through my shirt, leaving a wet spot when he moved to my other breast. "Tell me you're coming home, Vi."

I moaned as he slid his hand into my pants and underwear to cup my ass. His finger danced over my rosebud, teasing me with just enough pressure each time the tip of his finger pushed inside me.

"Tell me, Violet. Not just for the night, but forever." He raked his teeth over my neck to get my attention, but the sensation made my eyes roll. "You're ours. Say it."

His finger pushed in deeper and I threw my head back to moan at the ceiling. "I'm yours! I want to come back home!"

The sound of doors closing barely broke through my lust-filled daze. Ben's voice suddenly filling the car got my attention, though. "You're goddamn right you're coming back home."

I was left tingling and needy when Mason put me back in my own seat and buckled me in. I whined and squeezed my thighs together. "Fine. We'll come back to the house over the garage."

Justin shook his head. "You'll come to the main house."

"You're all so damn bossy. I'm an adult." I didn't know why I was arguing. I wanted to move in with them. I wanted to be a family.

Mason moved to the middle seat and buckled himself in again. "A friendly bet? If I win, you move into the main house. If you win, you choose where you want to go."

"What's the game?"

"Whoever lasts the longest wins." He reached over and cupped my sex. "I do you, you do me."

"Deal." I was going to shatter almost immediately and we all knew it. It was my admission I wanted to move into the main house with them. That, and I was dying to touch Mason.

I shoved my pants down to my knees and watched as he did the same. Once his erection was free and straining skywards, I gripped it tight and began stroking it.

He grunted and slid his hand between my thighs. His long fingers slid through my wetness and hooked into me. His palm ground against my clit and he leaned over to whisper to me. "I can't wait for you to sleep in our bed every night. You're going to wake up with my face buried in your sweet pussy every day. Every night you're going to be fucked in every way imaginable."

My toes curled and I pumped him faster. I was already so close.

"I can feel you squeezing my fingers. Let me have your

come. Give it to me, Vi." Mason growled just under his breath and then curled his fingers. As my orgasm hit, he leaned in closer and let out a low chuckle against my ear. "You're moving in, sweetheart."

I unbuckled my seatbelt and maneuvered so I could lower my face over his lap. Still holding the base of his shaft, I took him into my mouth and sucked.

"Goddammit, get her back in her seatbelt." Ben's growl was thick with lust.

I took as much of Mason's length in my mouth as I could and stroked the underside with my tongue before lifting my mouth again. I repeated that over and over while he grabbed a fistful of my hair and swore.

"Pull over." Justin's words came just before the truck came to an abrupt stop. The overhead light went on when a door was opened and then the door behind me opened and Justin was there, grabbing my hips and burying his tongue into me from behind.

I cried out around Mason's dick and sucked harder as Justin licked me from my clit to my ass. He growled into my lower lips and gripped my ass in his hands. He spread me out and then licked my ass until I was arching my back and panting. Each time I lifted my mouth from Mason's shaft to take a breath, he rubbed his precum over my lips and breathed my name like a curse.

"Car." Ben's warning worked on the guys. Justin took one last lick of me before pulling away and shutting the door. Mason made a sound of pure misery as he pulled me off of him and forced me into my seatbelt. "We'll be home in ten minutes."

I shifted in my seat and whimpered. I was so turned on I wasn't sure if I could make it ten seconds, much less ten minutes. "I'm not going to make it."

Mason grunted from beside me. "You're going to be fucked senseless the second he pulls into the garage."

I kicked my pants the rest of the way off and started working on my shirt until Mason stopped me. "What? I'm trying to be helpful."

He gripped my thigh and groaned. "No one else gets to see you."

My blood rushed through my body like lava. "Because I'm yours?"

Ben took a turn fast enough that I swung into Mason with a wild laugh. Mason caught me and nodded. "Because you're ours. Now say it like you mean it."

I bit my lip and lifted my shoulder in a coy shrug. "Make me."

CHAPTER 45
Ben

The garage door wasn't all the way down before I had Violet out of the truck and pressed against it. "Did I hear you say what I think you said?"

She gripped my shirt and yanked it over my head. "Depends on what you think you heard."

I spun her around and bent her over the workbench which stretched the length of the garage. In just her t-shirt, the bottom curve of her ass was out and I was quick to push the shirt the rest of the way up her back. "It sounded a lot like you daring us to make you admit who you belong to. That's a dangerous game, though, Vi. We haven't touched you in over a month and we've desperately missed you. You're also teasing men who thought they'd lost you. Are you sure you want to play that game?"

She opened her mouth to answer and I spanked her bare ass hard enough to leave my handprint on her silky skin. She yelped but pressed her ass back into me. "Make me. Fuck me out of my head so I can take what I want.

Please."

I spanked her again and then pulled her up so I could take her mouth in a fierce kiss. She ran her hands over me until Mason stepped up behind her and pinned her arms behind her back. I felt her breath hitch and eased back to look at her.

Justin pressed his mouth just under her ear and whispered. "Hold still."

Violet watched as he took a pair of the shears we kept in the garage and cut her shirt down the middle. Slow and steady, he let his knuckles drag over her skin as he went. Her pupils were dilated and I could smell the arousal dripping down her thighs. She was as needy for us as we were for her.

She'd tried to deny us, though. I wanted to punish her for pushing us away. She'd hurt herself on top of what we'd done by not letting us take care of her.

"On your knees, Violet." I watched as she dropped down immediately and then looked up at me with wide eyes and hungrily parted lips. "Crawl into the house. Let us watch you on your hands and knees."

Mason cut his eyes to me and I knew he was worried I was pushing her too far. Justin kept his eyes on Violet, gauging her reaction every step of the way.

Violet held my gaze and a slow smirk lifted her mouth. Without a word, she went down on her hands and began the slowest, most sensual crawl I'd ever imagined possible. I realized instantly she'd turned it into a punishment for me having the audacity to make her crawl around. It just turned me on more to know she wasn't going to bend to my will, just because. If it meant her pleasure, she'd do it every time. But crawling because I wanted her to? She wasn't doing it.

I followed along behind her like a lost dog, loving the view she made. I could see the shine of her juices coating her pussy and thighs and the way her waist nipped in called to my hands. Her hair hung over one shoulder but then she looked back at us and flipped her hair to the other side and her breasts swayed from the movement. It was heaven and hell. It was seduction and torture.

I couldn't take anymore, so once she was in the house, I picked her up and carried her into the living room. Positioning her so she was bent over the back of the couch, I went around to the other side and pulled a chair closer so I was right across from her. Like I knew they would, Mason and Justin were on her in an instant. They stroked every part of her they could and kissed her from her ankles to her ears.

Violet held my gaze, even as she shook from her desire. She was panting as Mason fingered her and Justin tugged at her nipples. I stood up and leaned over the couch so we were face to face. She licked her lips and moaned when Mason's fingers pressed into her ass.

"You belong here. You belong with us." I ran my thumb over her lips and then pinched her chin so she couldn't look away. "You get mad? You do it here. You get sad? You do it here. You get needy? You do it here. With us. No more running from us."

Her face pinched and I smiled when I saw that Mason had eased another finger into her ass. "You can't leave…like that."

I ran my hand down to her throat and stroked her soft skin. "You have our word."

Mason lined his body up with hers and thrust his cock

deep, dragging out a long scream from her. He gripped her waist and went straight to fucking her hard and fast.

Violet dropped her head forward against my hand but Justin wrapped her hair around his hand and pulled her back up. Her breasts bounced with Mason's hard thrusts and she made little grunts with each one. Her cheeks had flushed red and her eyes weren't focused anymore.

"Who do you belong to, Violet?" I kissed her hard. "Say it."

When she still wouldn't, I sat back down in the chair in front of her. Her eyes stayed on me as I slowly unzipped my pants and pulled my dick out. Stroking it, I saw the way her eyes moved up and down with my hand. She licked her lips between moans.

Mason pulled out of her and backed away, his face twisted in pain. "Who do you belong to, Violet?"

She let out a frustrated growl. "You! I belong to the three of you! And you belong to me. Say you belong to me."

I was in front of her in the blink of an eye, kissing her deep. "Of course we fucking belong to you. We love you, Violet."

"What are you going to do about it?" The challenge in her voice spurred me on. She knew it, too.

Holding her face in my hands, I gazed into her eyes and rose to her challenge. "Marry you and have a dozen babies."

Her eyes widened and then a bright smile stretched across her face. "I'll say yes if someone makes me come in the next two minutes."

She was pinned between Justin and Mason on the couch almost instantly, being stretched as they both fucked her. I stood next to the couch and she arched her body so she could offer me her mouth. I took it gladly. I slid in deep and watched her eyes flutter shut while I felt her moans and screams around my length. She was already coming.

Justin was under her, taking her hard from below. Mason took her ass from above her and he was riding her hard. We were all racing towards our release after being apart for too long. The sounds of our groans and curses filled the room. Violet sucked me harder as she came and I was fucked. I was the first to come and I filled her mouth and watched her struggle to swallow all of me.

Mason went next, filling her ass as he shouted her name. Justin followed quickly behind and like lightning, we were burned out as fast as we'd started.

The three of them lay as they were until Violet grunted and struggled out from between them. That had Justin and Mason stretching out on opposite ends of the couch as Violet curled into my lap in the chair and draped herself over me.

We were all quiet as we caught our breaths and recovered. Finally, when my breathing slowed, I laughed.

Violet lifted her head from my chest and smiled. "What?"

"I think I let you goad me into proposing during a rough fucking." I shook my head. "I refuse to let that count."

She stretched her legs out and wrapped her arms around my neck. "It counts."

"That's not the story we're going to tell our kids, Vi." Mason shook his head. "Especially when only one of us was aware it was happening in that moment."

"Are you saying you *don't* want to marry me?"

Mason sat up. "Of course, I want to marry you, Vi."

She giggled. "Okay, fine. I'll marry you. Don't beg."

Justin shot me a look and I narrowed my eyes at him. The bastard was about to make me and Mason look like idiots. I could just feel it. He reached into his pants pocket and knelt in front of her with a diamond ring. "I was going to wait, but I've been ready since the day we met you, Violet. Marry us. Make us the happiest men alive. Promise us forever in front of our son. I love you, Violet. Will you marry us?"

She leapt into his arms and tackled him to the floor. Covering his face in kisses, she finally sat up while straddling him and held out her hand. "Yes! I'll marry you."

I shook my head at Mason and jerked my thumb at Justin. "Of course, he already has a ring."

"Mr. Boy Scout. He was just waiting for the chance to show us up." Mason grinned and fell back on the couch. "Bested by my own best friend."

Violet got up and stood in front of us, as naked as the day she was born. "I have two things to say to you guys right now."

I smiled up at her. "Go on."

"First, I'm starving. Seeing that you guys are safe and still in functioning order has given me my appetite back." She squirmed in place. "Second... I need to pee and since I have about five hundred sticks to pee on, maybe someone could grab a handful for me?"

Fifteen minutes later, we were still lining up tests on the bathroom counter while Violet ate a cup of mac and cheese perched on the closed toilet. She'd peed in a cup and was letting us do the rest of the work. She was adorable in my t-shirt and nothing else. Her hair was a mess and she was eating like she hadn't in days.

I was just opening my mouth to lecture her about eating more when the first timer went off. Justin, Mason, and I all panicked and in our search to find which stick had been first, we knocked half of them onto the floor, spilled the cup of pee, and somehow had four timers going off on three phones all at the same time.

Violet took another bite of her mac and cheese and held up a test. She giggled at us and turned it around so we could see the results. Positive.

EPILOGUE
Violet

Nine Months Later

"I don't know... I mean, yes, she's a girl, but she's also two months old. I don't know if *Doll's* is the best place for her to be. What if she grows up staring at dildos and it does something to her?" I held Delilah to my chest as she fed and ran my finger over her soft hair. "It's so crazy to me she came out with a head full of hair. Forrest was bald until he was ten months old, I swear."

Joanie wiggled her fingers and fought the need to hold Delilah. "I think our little angel is going to grow up with a very progressive viewpoint on sex, no matter what she sees in here."

Margaret stormed into *Doll's* with pink war paint on her cheeks. "After nearly a year of putting it off, Mayor Stevens has agreed to put the battle on the town calendar. It's finally happening."

I glanced over at Joanie and we both rolled our eyes. Mayor Stevens had been backing out of the battle for one reason or another since the beginning. I'd grown an entire child and he was still making excuses.

"I don't think it's a coincidence he's more confident to hold the games now that there are more men in town. Men who are built like gods and who seem to be very interested in our special little diner in town." Margaret wagged her eyebrows at Joanie. "Anything you want to add to this conversation?"

Joanie's face had flushed a deep red and she shook her head. "Nope. Not a thing."

My phone rang and I looked down to see it was Justin. I stood up and walked to a corner of the room to answer. "Hey! Is everything okay? How's Forrest?"

"Everything's fine, baby. Forrest is great. He's caught a bunch of fish already." Justin and the guys had taken my dad and Forrest on a fishing trip for the day and I was a little nervous about Forrest being on the river. The guys weren't worried about him at all, though. They'd already instilled so much knowledge and confidence in him that he barely seemed like the same kid. He mimicked almost everything they did and acted so much older than seven. That part killed me. I wanted him to be my baby forever.

"Are you taking lots of pictures?" I gently bounced Delilah. "If you feel like it's too many, take more."

"I've got plenty. I promise." I could hear the smile in his voice. "Hey, your dad mentioned that he was going to take Forrest home with him tonight. Is there something we forgot about?"

I grinned at the wall of toys in front of me. "Nope. My parents wanted to spend some time with him, so they asked if he could sleep over."

"How's Delilah?"

"She's eating right now, so she's great. I've officially shown my boobs to most of Lilyfield in an attempt to keep your daughter fed. I think she's a black hole."

Justin growled. "Violet…"

I pretended to not know what he was going on about. "What? She is. Just this morning, I was at the diner and she wouldn't stop fussing until I fed her. Half of the training center was there, I swear. Of course, Delilah kicked the blanket off before she latched on so a few dozen soldiers got the full nip and everything today."

"Violet, you'd better be kidding."

I lowered my voice. "And if I'm not?"

"We'll be home after dinner. You may not be cleared for sex yet but that doesn't mean I can't tease you until you scream." He groaned. "You're going to make me kill a bunch of innocent men one day, Vi. You're playing with fire."

"I'll do my best not to flash any more handsome soldiers before you get home. I love you!" I hung up and turned around to find Joanie shaking her head at me. "What?"

"You're awful to them. You tease those poor men nonstop." She grinned. "Keep up the good work."

I walked with her out of *Doll's* and into *Good, Clean Fun*. "I had a secret doctor's appointment yesterday. I've been cleared for sex. Dr. Morgan told me not to do anything too insane, but she said to just listen to my body, so I'm going to listen to my body sing my guys' praises all night tonight. My parents are keeping Forrest and Delilah."

"How are the guys going to handle a night without the baby?" She knew how much they hovered over both Forrest and Delilah.

"I plan on being naked in the driveway when they get home. They're going to lose their minds." I laughed at Joanie's shocked expression. "No one will see me but them! And it'll still have the desired effect of making them insane and distracting them from missing the kids."

"You're wild. I never would've known when you first showed up that you would be so off your rocker. You seemed so sweet and shy." Joanie stopped with me outside *The One and Only* and glanced inside. "You know… When I moved to Lilyfield, I thought I'd escaped asshole men with asshole attitudes and asshole bodies."

I followed her gaze and saw Chase sitting with two other men. They were business partners of his from what I could tell. They were all so private that I didn't know anything about them. "They're still bothering you about expanding?"

"About everything." She saw Chase looking at her and flipped him off before turning her back to him. "If Ted Bundy asked me over to help him load his van, I'd do it over spending one more minute with that jerk."

"Have you thought about asking Margaret for help? Or Coco? I feel like Coco would know how to handle them." I watched her face light up. "Yeah, you go talk to them. I'm going to go home and shave every inch of my body."

She sighed dramatically. "You have the best life."

I nodded. "I really do."

"No, *you* have the best life, Joanie." She mocked me saying it back to her with all kinds of sass and then threw her hands in the air just as Chase walked up behind her. Her hand connected with his nose and they were both instantly at each other's throats.

"Bye!" I hurried away to avoid another one of their

fights. Personally, I thought they just needed to have sex and get it over with. That might've just been my sex deprived brain, though.

I decided to really mess with the guys one more time before they got home. I wanted them at the end of their control. I sent a quick picture of myself, still feeding Delilah, making sure to include people walking in the background. I didn't say anything, but I didn't have to. The top curve of my breast was out and I knew the guys would be going crazy.

Almost instantly, I got a text back from Ben.

You're ours.

I sent him a response before slipping my phone into my purse and hurrying home.

Prove it.

The End.

THANK YOU

Thank you for sticking with 'Second Chance SEALs Next Door' right to the end – I hope it was a mission you enjoyed! If you found yourself laughing, sighing, or even rolling your eyes at the antics of our charming SEALs and the fiery spirit of Violet, then consider yourself a part of the SEALs Squad. Did you secretly wish for an underwater rescue or a twist where everyone turns out to be undercover spies? Hang tight; the next adventure might just surprise you!

Your support is more valuable to me than a secret SEALs debriefing. Whether this book brought a smile to your face, a tear to your eye, or simply offered a fun escape during a coffee break, I'm thrilled to have shared this story with you.

Keep your eyes peeled – there's more excitement, romance, and maybe a few unexpected plot twists ahead (shh, that's classified).

A toast to you, the best part of this storytelling journey!

Cheers,
Summer Haze

ABOUT THE AUTHOR

Meet Summer Haze, a laughter-loving scribe of sizzling reverse harem romances. Scribbling from sunny California, she's your go-to gal for reverse harem love stories that'll make you snort-giggle while you fan yourself. When she's not crafting tales of brooding billionaires and nannies with nerves of steel, you'll find her striking yoga poses, rescuing cute puppies, or experimenting with the limits of her coffee machine.

In the spirit of brevity: Summer writes. You laugh. Hearts flutter. Ready for the rom-com ride of your life? Prepare your funny bone and heartstrings to be thoroughly tickled.

Printed in Great Britain
by Amazon